Viroids

Writers Apex

Gateway Towards Success

8063 MADISON AVE #1252
Indianapolis, IN 46227
+13176596889
www.writersapex.com

VIROIDS

CLEMENT S. MASLOFF

Part I.

I.

What sort of assignment was this going to be? worried and wondered Investigative Inspector Skopo Kitanin.

First of all, he had to locate the office of the Chief Librarian.

It was years since as a student at Police College he had been in this high, enormous hall with its rows of reading viewers mounted on polymetal tables. Only a few scattered users were seated about the place this early in the morning. The most dedicated ones, decided the police officer. As quiet as a sleeping chamber, he told himself.

Skopo caught sight of what he was searching for at the far end of the great reading room. A closed black door, with a thin young man sitting at a desk beside it, like an unarmed guard. He raised his eyes from the smaller reader device in front of him and stared at the stranger in a dark business suit for a moment.

"Can I help you?" he murmured in a sweet, pleasant tenor voice.

The detective, a tall, husky figure with dark brown eyes and hair, leaned forward to whisper to the secretary. "I have an appointment to see the director."

The woman's name was Totmax, Skopo had learned back at headquarters. She had only recently become head of the Central Library of Kalender. And the trouble there had begun at once, as if she had brought it there with her. The holding institution had started to suffer erasure of written and printed books and documents at once. Valuable parts of the library's collections had vanished as if they had never been there or even existed.

"Follow me," said the wiry aide to Skopo, rising from his secretarial desk and stepping to the black door, opening it for the visitor.

The investigator made his way slowly into the old-fashioned, spacious office. The gatekeeper entered behind him, closing the polymetal door behind him.

At a long working table sat a middle-aged woman with a concerned, serious face. She was the first to speak.

"Sit down, Investigative Inspector Kitanin." Her right arm indicated a wire chair in front of her.

"I want you here too, Mlem," she told her assistant.

The two males took chairs across from Dari Totmax, whose penetrating dark eyes were already examining the impassive face of the detective.

Years of experience had taught Skopo to keep a mask of stone while on the job.

"Shall we get down to business, sir?" proposed the director.

"That would be best," replied Kitanin.

"My brother, Mlem, will describe for you how this business began."

She nodded in the direction of the young man who worked as her secretary.

The latter pivoted toward Skopo. "I was first to discover this erasure damage. One evening, about three weeks ago, I noticed a reading viewer that was still on. The screen was blank, although a viroid ribbon was still being projected onto the surface from the memory depository downstairs. It was surprising and disturbed me."

Skopo stared fixedly at the slight, scholarly-looking brother who served as his sister's aide.

"Did you try to find out who had used the reading device last?"

"Of course, I did," frowned Mlem Totmax. "But that trail led nowhere."

At this point, the director interrupted.

"Unfortunately, there is no way we can identify the user of that particular viewer. Our machines are available for free to the general reading public. This is not a library from the distant past, where one can withdraw cellulose or paper books. There is nothing here for a thief to steal. All of our records, archives, documents, and collections are recorded on virus in our memory banks below this building. Our central storehouse is open to all who wish to use it. How can we deal with a form of vandalism that has never occurred before and is impossible to explain?"

"Can something be secretly brought in to wipe out particular viroid memories? Some sort of new, unknown instrument that is able to cause this damage?" As Skopo spoke, he studied the eyes of Dari Totmax, as impenetrable as a black diamond. Her face seemed to give off a soft, golden glow. She was a unique, peculiar individual, he realized.

"I know of no technology that can accomplish such viral erasure, Mr. Kitanin," murmured the director. "There has been nothing like this since viral recording and memory was first developed and placed in use."

"You did not call for police assistance till now," declared Skopo. "This vandalism has gone on for over a fortnight already. Am I correct?"

"Yes," admitted Dari with evident regret. "We should not have hesitated that long. I recognize that fact. Our hope was that the damage would end on its own. That was our idea, but it proved an empty one. The erasures continue to the present day."

"The number of viroid ribbons ruined has risen higher and higher," added her brother in a pensive tone. "This can grow into an unprecedented disaster for the Library. The cost to our archives and collections will be irreparable."

The detective looked sharply at him, then turned to his sister.

"Is there any pattern in what is being attacked and destroyed?" he inquired. "What sort of material is the target of erasures?"

"Nothing specific is destroyed," groaned the director. "Erasure can occur to any viroid ribbon, of any character. There is nothing specially selected, nothing excluded."

    VIROIDS

"That is an interesting point to consider," thoughtfully mumbled the detective.

Dari stared at him with apprehension. "Our entire library is at risk if this continues to spread and widen."

For a few moments, there was silence.

"It's best I get to work on the case at once," said Skopo as he rose to his feet. "My plan is to pose as a user of one of your public viewers. The purpose will be to keep an eye on what the others are up to inside the reading hall."

The director turned her head toward her brother and addressed him.

"Find a vacant position for Inspector Kitanin and show him how to operate the viewer, Mlem. Be sure that there are no signs indicating anything special is going on with him."

The aide nodded that he understood what was required of him.

"Thank you both," muttered Skopo as he headed for the black polymetal door of the director's office.

II.

The detective occasionally scanned the huge hall for suspicious activity.

His viewer was on a table close to the entrance, at the opposite end from the director's office and the secretary's desk. It was possible for Kitanin to see anyone who entered or exited. Since every other reader was facing away from him, his eyes took in all the other positions while he himself remained unseen.

Since he had to appear to be a legitimate patron of the viral library, Skopo punched in the index number of a popular volume he had heard of and was aware of, "The Historical Development of Viral Technology".

From time to time, he took limited glances at the first page of the text on the green silver screen in front of him. He found some items that drew his interest.

"The origins of viroid ribbon and memory lie in a jungle of legal dispute and argument. Perhaps the whole truth will never be established with finality.

"The laboratory of the Virtek Company is the actual birthplace, according to the partisans of that corporation. Half a dozen of its research scientists have claimed the honor of having been the first. Counterclaims to Virtek by the independent pioneer Zado Atat were rejected in the courts. Technical patents went to Virtek for the work of its sextet of researchers. Atat died in abject poverty, an ambitious recluse, forgotten in the new world of advanced viral science."

Skopo looked up and made a quick survey of the other reading tables. His eyes stopped at one lone figure next to the left wall of the big hall. It took him a moment to realize what it was that riveted his attention there.

A short, shabby man with a long wand in his hand was silently rubbing it against his viewer screen.

This had to be the vandal erasing viral memory, Skopo told himself with rising excitement.

Would it be wise to make an arrest at once? No. The best strategy at this point was to wait and tail this suspect. A wider net might capture possible confederates along with this particular criminal.

The detective switched off his viewer and rose from the table.

Silently, he made his way out of the reading hall, out through the entrance, then down the front steps into Library Square.

Skopo sat down on a rubber street bench and patiently waited.

After about five minutes, the round little man he was interest in came out of the building. It will be easy to follow a person wearing such a reddish orange suit, decided the detective. It seemed best to give him a head start, then follow at the maximum possible distance. Experience had made Kitanin an excellent stalker through the winding, narrow streets of Kalender. Here in the ancient central district of the city, motor vehicles were prohibited. The narrow walkways belonged to pedestrians alone. Following someone here was easy under such circumstances.

The investigator knew well the streets, alleys, and lanes of the old quarter.

Few people were about at this time, it appeared. The suspect's pace was a brisk one. Where had he hidden his wand-like stick? wondered Skopo.

On both sides of the narrow street were small specialty shops huddled together on the ground floors of large blocks of apartments. Shoes, carpets, jewelry, luggage, furniture suits and dresses, and viral tapes and equipment were for sale in different stores.

While he ambled along with energy, the pursuer kept his eyes fixed on the red-orange cloth far ahead of him. The target appeared in a hurry to get somewhere. He did not look back once to see if anyone were shadowing him. Why was he rushing so swiftly to a destination? What was the reason for such haste?

Suddenly, there was no one ahead of Skopo.

The quarry must have lurched into a side street or lane. The detective started to accelerate until he was moving at nearly a run. Had he lost the trail of a culprit? That would mean having to start over again, trying to find the vandal at the library at a future time. This particular hunt had turned into failure.

As he made a turn into the side lane, the policeman smiled ruefully.

Might as well stop, for the subject he was following had vanished from sight.

Skopo did not panic, for past experiences had taught Skopo not to despair when something like this happened. He knew that such defeats were possible.

He looked up and down the shadow-filled lane.

How far could the suspect have gone? What was the most likely business or building he could have entered?

The stalker's attention focused on a transmetal door to a small restaurant.

"Carnivan" proclaimed the gas sign on the red brick outside wall of the place. This was a carnivorous eatery with an attached meat market behind it.

Kitanin walked up and looked in one of the wide front windows.

Patrons sat at circular tables, eating and conversing. A long lunch-counter took up the left wall of the restaurant. In the rear were displays of meats for sale. Shelves with milk, butter, and eggs were available.

As his eyes returned to where people were sitting and eating, Skopo fixed his eyes upon one of the waiters coming out of the kitchen in the back with a tray of non-vegetarian foods. The small, tubby man wore an immaculate white apron, yet the detective instantly recognized him.

The vandal he had trailed worked here, serving the radical minority of carnivores in Kalender.

Perhaps the criminal is a flesh-eater, frowned the investigator, himself a vegetarian in a society and culture that frowned upon and avoided all forms of meat.

This case was becoming strange, Skopo said to himself.

III.

Mlem Totmax was watching the green lines of letters on the screen in front of him and only looked away when Skopo was inches away from him.

"Where have you been?" whispered the secretary. "It was over an hour ago that you walked out of the reading hall."

The investigator leaned forward. "I must talk with your sister. You too, should hear what I have to report."

Mlem sprang to his feet and stepped to the black door, opening it for the police officer, then entering the office behind him. Dari, working at reports on her viewer, gave a start upon seeing Kitanin. "Has anything happened?" she said with alarm in her voice.

Then, thinking again, she invited the visitor to take a seat across from her.

"There has been a major development," announced Skopo. "Only time will tell if it will bring this whole affair to a conclusion." He went on to describe his pursuit of the man with the wand-stick. When this was finished, Dari turned and spoke to Mlem.

"Will you find out if there has been any memory destruction today?"

Without a word, the brother rose and slipped out of the office.

Skopo stared intently at the library director. Finally, he asked her a question.

"Have you ever had any trouble with carnivores in this institution?"

Dari shook her head. "No. I can't think of any reason for problems with meat-eaters at the Central Library. We take no position on dietary rules or customs."

"I see," muttered the other.

"The erasures have been completely random," she added. "No particular subject matter has been picked out for special attention or treatment by the vandal or vandals involved."

"Yes," nodded Skopo. "There may be others in this beyond the waiter whom I tailed out of here today."

A short silence followed.

"What do you plan to do next?" inquired Dari.

"I will return to the Carnivan for dinner, although I have never tasted animal food in any form at all."

"It will be a new experience for you?" she grinned with sympathy.

"Indeed. It is best to move slowly in this area. I will easily reveal myself a neophyte, one with no experience beyond a vegetarian diet. My order must be for something simple and easy to digest."

"You mean to find out the identity of this waiter?"

"Yes. If he is the one who serves me dinner, it will give me an opening to talk with the man and hopefully learn more about him."

A sudden idea struck Dari. "I want to go with you to this restaurant," she proposed with determination and spirit. "It would appear much more natural, a pair rather than a single patron. Perhaps as we talk back and forth between ourselves, we can entice the waiter to reveal things about himself."

For a moment, Skopo considered the proposal.

"It might help put him off his guard," he said, overcoming his initial reluctance and relenting.

"Very well, then. We will visit the Carnavan together. Are you familiar with this type of food, Miss Totmax?"

"No," she replied. "Like you, I grew up a strict vegetarian."

The two proceeded to make their plans for that evening.

❖ ❖ ❖

Two persons ambled along in the dimming twilight, their pace slow and leisurely. There was nothing about either worthy of notice.

People going home from work or on their way to evening recreation passed them in both directions. Lighting tubes on the outside of high apartments began to turn on. Restaurants began to fill up with hungry customers.

"Don't be afraid to talk to the waiter," murmured Skopo under his breath. "He should be off guard at his job."

Dari peered down at the weathered cobblestones ahead of them.

"What sort of monster would commit an act like today's?" she asked with an exasperated sigh. "We can never replace the original literary sources that man erased. The loss is a permanent one."

They advanced a short distance, then entered a side street. "This is where the non-vegan restaurant is, Miss Totmax."

"Please call me Dari," she softly suggested to him.

As purple dusk gathered outside, they stepped into the brightly lit restaurant section of the Carnavan. Most of the round tables appeared occupied. But since the dinner hour was coming to an end, the place should be less crowded from now on, Skopo calculated. He motioned with his hand to a vacant table near the door to the kitchen. Dari led the way there.

The couple sat down opposite each other. Neither of them spoke.

A silky voice startled them. "I'll be with you in just a moment."

Both of the newly arrived glanced at the tray-carrying waiter passing swiftly past their table. Short and lumpy, he wore a large white apron of cotton.

Skopo signaled to Dari with a blink of the eye. Yes, this was the one they were interested in. The librarian pursed her mouth. She understood perfectly.

Shortly, the stubby little waiter approached their table. He handed each of them a small menu. "Do you wish to order immediately or later?" his high tenor asked.

"We are new to carnivorous fare," explained the detective with exaggerated hesitancy and embarrassment. "Neither of us has eaten in

 VIROIDS

here before. Perhaps you could recommend a good selection for us to start with." He stared at the waiter, his eyes begging for guidance.

"Yes, of course," was the fluttering answer. "I would suggest you start with soup. Our most popular one is made with chicken and eggs. Garlic, pepper, and onion are in it for taste. Then, for the main dish, I myself would order the roasted lamb cutlet, covered with special cream sauce. There is a lot of animal protein in all of it. Your mouth will water as soon as you sniff this meat."

Skopo felt his stomach turn over. "Very well," he forced himself to agree.

"I will have the same," added Dari. "It sounds good to me."

The waiter appeared transported. "And for desert, I recommend our genuine ice cream made of imported cow's milk. It is high in animal fat, you know."

"Yes," agreed Kitanin. "That sounds like just what we came here for. We are only recent adherents of the meat-based diet. There are many animal foods that neither of us have ever tried."

"It takes time to adjust to a new way of eating," the waiter explained. "Many beginning carnivores have trouble fully adjusting. Some suffer from sudden lapses into their old ways. I myself once had a severe panic attack, but recovered and returned to eating flesh. For people here on our planet of Farmer, it isn't easy to break away from the old rules and superstitions of the past. But I try the best that I can, increasing my consumption of meat each day, each week that passes."

He took their menus and hurried off to the kitchen.

Skopo and his companion exchanged glances, but neither said anything to the other. Their communication was an intangible kind.

✦ ✦ ✦

By the time the pair finished their desert, the restaurant was only half full. When the waiter brought their bill, both appeared well satisfied.

"I hope that both of you enjoyed the meal," he told them cheerfully. "Perhaps our expert cooking will convince you that an animal diet is the only true one for humans to follow."

The detective gave him a sharp, steady look. "As you said earlier, it is easy to backslide from meat consumption when one is new to it. If only we could get together with other carnivores for mutual support and guidance, that might save us from pain and suffering."

All at once, the waiter seemed to grab the bait offered him by Skopo.. He leaned forward so that both customers could hear his whispered words. His face was flushed with excitement.

"My name is Trepo," he softly muttered. "I am active in a group that helps its members learn more about pure animal nutrition. It encourages the individual not to slide or stray back to vegetarianism. Each of us provides moral support to the others.

"Would you two be interested in attending one of our meetings and lectures?"

"Very much so," responded Kitanin with enthusiasm.

"That goes for me, too," added Dari.

"I'll write down the time and location for you," grinned Trepo. "If anyone should ask who you are, tell them you know the main speaker for the evening, Trepo Lenad. That is me."

The waiter took a blank check from the pad he carried and wrote out what he had promised to. "I shall be expecting you at my lecture, then," he smiled as he left their table.

IV.

The two made their way slowly through the crowded night streets.

Why do so many inhabitants of Kalender prefer the outside to their homes and apartments? wondered Skopo. Was it due to boredom with life indoors? What did people think they would find in the evening streets?

Perhaps the sense of being among so many happy strangers gave an emotional lift to persons who had a humdrum existence during the day. Strangers represented pure potential to each other. You to me, I to you. Even the poor can pose as something they are not. Each one can imagine another life, different from their familiar one.

So mused Skopo as the pair reached Library Square.

"Why don't you come to our apartment?" proposed Dari out of the blue. "Mlem is waiting for me there. You can tell him yourself what happened. And we can lay down our plans for the carnivore meeting we will be attending together."

* * *

The flat was on the tenth floor of an ordinary-looking old rockstone building in the bohemian quarter of Kalender.

A lifter carried Dari and the detective slowly upward, with a half dozen other passengers who got off before them.

Mlem opened the door and welcomed the two in.

Dari explained "I invited our friend to stop in so all three of us can discuss what happened tonight and what comes next."

"Sit down, please," Mlem invited their visitor.

Skopo took a large velvet sofa chair made of soft rubber. Brother and sister sat down on opposite ends of a long stuffed couch from an earlier time that they had inherited from their parents.

"This couch belonged to our mother and father," explained Mlem. "At one time, our family owned a farm outside Kalender. But the city expanded and swallowed up their rural area."

Dari continued the story. "They were amaranth farmers as their ancestors had been since coming to planet Farmer. Vegetarianism was at the foundation of their lives. Like almost all growers, they raised no animals and consumed no meat. Is it this great city that creates carnivores, Skopo?"

"I never thought of it that way," confessed the latter. "The craving for animal food is a very new development on Farmer, a sort of fad or craze."

"It seems to be spreading and strengthening," noted Mlem.

Dari proceeded to describe what happened at the restaurant for her brother. Then, she turned to the detective with a question.

"Do you suppose that carnivorous motives lie behind the vandalism at the Central Library?" she boldly asked him.

"It's too early to tell," cautioned Skopo. "We have to find out much more."

No one said a word for a short while, until Mlem asked a sudden question.

"How much danger is there, Mr. Kitanin, for you and my sister in attending this meeting of meat-eaters?"

Skopo focused his gaze on the brother. "I don't foresee any trouble," he answered reassuringly. "There is little chance that our identities will be known by anyone present. Besides, I always enter anywhere prepared for the worst." He reached into the inside pocket of his purple coat and drew out a small, transparent object. "This is a polyplastic shooter that serves as my final defense."

The weapon went back into its hiding place over his heart.

Dari was next to speak. "I feel perfectly safe being with Skopo," she murmured with confidence. "This waiter suspects nothing." Her eyes turned to the detective. "Isn't that correct?" she asked him.

"Yes," he strongly replied. "I am sure that any trouble can be handled by us."

"Then, if that is the situation, I intend to accompany the two of you," asserted Mlem with a smile. "There is no reason the three of us should not go there as a group, is there?"

Dari seemed surprised and shaken. "I don't think you ought to come," she protested with emotion. "Trepo will be expecting only the two he met at the Carnavan. Your presence would have to fbe explained by us."

Her brother decided to appeal to Skopo to arbitrate the matter.

"What is your opinion, Skopo?" he pleaded. "Don't you think three persons can snoop much better than only two?"

The investigator thought a moment before responding to Mlem.

"The best cover is to tell as much of the truth as possible. That makes people willing to accept what you say, even the untrue parts. So if anyone asks for your name, give it. Admit working at the Central Library. I myself will be the sole liar among us three, claiming to be a new employee there. If pressed, I will admit being involved in fighting the recent vandal attacks."

It took a while for this stratagem to sink in for the Totmaxes. The detective explained it with calm patience.

"If I appear to be a protector of the library and falling into carnivorism, someone there may try to recruit me to the vandal side."

It was Mlem who reacted first.

"That is most clever. Make them believe you are a person who could be of great value if connected with their conspiracy."

Dari appeared lost in a puzzle over motive. "Why would a cult of extreme carnivorousness be committing crimes against our viral memory ribbons?"

"That is what we have to find out," muttered Skopo, thinking aloud. "Can you have lunch with me tomorrow at the Carnavan, Dari? It would impress Trepo that we are serious about joining his movement."

"Certainly. But won't you be watching out for erasures at the Library>"

Kitanin frowned. "No. We have to give Trepo some breathing room. For a time, he must be allowed to destroy memory unhindered. I don't want him to suspect that anyone is on to what he is doing in the reading hall."

Dari was still worried. "What if my brother or I make a slip of some sort?"

The detective smiled at her. "I can always extricate us from the situation," he promised. "Remember, there is a weapon in my coat pocket."

"I'll be there, too," interjected Mlem. "If trouble occurs, there will be the three of us."

Skopo laughed. "We will keep you in reserve, my friend. I don't anticipate our unmasking in any way."

V.

On their way to lunch at the Carnavan, the investigator described to Dari what he had read that morning in the Kalender Morning News.

"They report that there has occurred the unexplained destruction of a financial page that was planned to be published today. The viroid matrix over which it is composed became totally blank. Business and financial circles have lost valuable information necessary for their operations. Viral experts are unable to explain what happened. Fears of greater mischief have arisen."

"There is a truly evil influence involved, I fear," said Dari in a whisper. "This is much more than the mad vandalism of a single lunatic."

Her companion glanced at Dari. "Yes, I agree."

A premonition of complicated conspiracy had been an early feeling in his mind, recalled the investigator. How far did it reach? he mused as they entered the now familiar side street.

The pair remained silent until they were inside the carnivorous restaurant. They stood for a moment, looking about. The lunchtime crowd seemed to have thinned out. A vacant table adjacent to the one they had occupied the previous evening attracted their attention. Dari nodded to Skopo. That was the place for them to be.

After sitting down, they waited patiently for Trepo to appear. Instead, an unfamiliar waiter came to their table.

"Good afternoon," crooned a lanky, bald-headed man in an apron. He gave each of them a menu. "Do you wish to order something immediately?"

The customers stared at each other a moment. This was unexpected, both of them recognized. Dari decided to take the initiative to straighten matters out.

"We haven't seen Trepo," she pleasantly chirped. "Is he still in the kitchen?"

The server grinned. "Are you friends of his?"

"Yes," interrupted Skopo. "We expected to see him, but it appears he is not here."

"He isn't. Trepo asked to have the day off."

"The entire day?" said the detective.

"That's right," confirmed the tall waiter. "He said that it was impossible for him to be here because of his father's condition. The old man is extremely ill and needs constant care and attention. At least that is what Trepo claims."

The waiter's right eye winked knowingly.

"I've never met Trepo's father," continued Skopo, hoping to elicit more information. "What is the old fellow like?"

"He is not a carnivore," grimaced the server with disgust. "Trepo has failed to convert him. I remember hearing that he worked for years as a viral engineer."

"That is interesting," murmured the detective, almost to himself. He lowered his eyes to the menu in his hands. "What do you recommend we have for lunch today?" he asked, raising his voice.

"Roast beef casserole," suggested the waiter with a smile. "It's one of the biggest favorites we have."

"I think I'll try that," ventured Dari.

"So will I," seconded her companion.

When the waiter was gone, Skopo whispered to the librarian.

"I'll run a background check on the Lenads, father and son. There may be something in the records about the one or the other."

❖ ❖ ❖

It was Mlem who opened the door to the apartment and let Skopo in.

"I looked through a lot of police sources on the console screen at my office," announced the investigator, standing in the living room. "There is interesting material available about the father of Trepo. I found out that Vrem Lenad lives with his son and is a viral engineer who specializes in linguistic applications. He is a Master of Technology who graduated from Kalender University and works for a language school as its chief engineer.

"Isn't that an interesting background?" grinned the visitor.

"Dari will find that useful to know," remarked the brother. "She will be here momentarily."

The two males sat down and waited for the appearance of the Library Director.

"There was alarming news on the virion line this morning," noted Skopo suddenly. "The broadcast that I caught mentioned that crop reports have suffered serious damage and interruptions overnight.

"And once again, stock market price quotations have undergone erasures and general ruination. Viral scientists who were called in proved unable to figure out how such attacks might have occurred.

"There appears to be some sort of unknown advanced but exotic new technology involved, but no one has the least knowledge how it could be accomplished."

"It would seem, then, that the Central Library is not the sole target or victim of these unidentified vandals," said Mlem with a deep sigh of vexation and frustration. "But yesterday there occurred several focused attacks that destroyed specific kind of content. There was a concentration upon erasing and wiping out specialized areas of advanced viral science."

At that moment, Dari emerged from her room in the rear of the apartment. She wore a linen dress with pink and yellow stripes on it.

"Good morning, Skopo," she melodically chirped.

The detective rose to his feet, smiling at her. She motioned him to sit down, then took a place beside her brother.

"I've told our friend about yesterday's library damage," muttered Mlem, a frown covering his brow.

"It grows daily," said his sister. "I hope we can stop it soon." Her eyes fixed on Skopo.

"The Central Library is no longer the only target," added the latter, proceeding to relate the virion line attacks on important broadcasts.

"This plague is spreading, then," sighed Dari. "Perhaps the Library damage was a sort of experimental dry run. My hope is that Trepo Lenad can open the right door for us. Did you find anything of value in his background or history?"

"Not much. His education ended abruptly at the University. He studied viral science but became a restaurant worker. I find his father much more interesting."

"Why is that?" exclaimed Dari, growing excited.

'He works as a viral engineer for an outfit called the Atat Language School. I would like to meet and question this man. His technical knowledge could be a basic, important factor in this erasure campaign we are witnessing. He may be at the very center of it all."

"The father is supposed to be ill, according to Trepo," remembered Dari.

Skopo pursed his thin lips. "That may or may not be so. It would be useful if we could convince Trepo to invite us to his flat. I would like to learn what this Vnem Lenad does as viral engineer at a language school."

"Was this place named for the crackpot crank who claimed he invented the viroid ribbon, the development that inspired much on our planet of Farmer?" interjected Mlem with curiosity.

All at once, the detective grasped the connection being made.

"You are referring to Zado Atat, I take it. He claimed to having been first to engrave micro-data on viroid tape, but his rivals at Virtek challenged, defeated, and humiliated him. I overlooked the significance of the school's name, Mlem."

The latter smiled with pride. "The name just rang a bell for me," he modestly noted.

"The waiter told us his father is not a practicing carnivore," recalled Dari. "But the son could be exercising extraordinary influence over him, for all we know."

"There are varying degrees of animal diet," explained Skopo. "An adherent may be only a lacto-carnivore who consumes milk, or a ovo-lacto one who eats eggs as well. A pesco-carnivore has a fish diet. The full carnivore diet takes in all forms of meat, milk, and eggs. It is the highest, purest group."

Mlem turned to his sister. "What do you intend to become. Dari?" he chuckled with a serious face. "Are you planning to go the whole route?"

The librarian gave him a withering look. "This is a dangerous business we are getting involved in," she chided him. "I think it best of we save our levity for later, when all of this is resolved."

"We have to be prepared to face problems and questions at the lecture by Trepo tonight," warned Skopo.

VI.

No more than thirty were present in the rented meeting hall when Skopo entered, Dari on his right, Mlem slightly behind them. The three took planewood chairs in the last row. The detective surveyed the audience without seeming to stare. Ordinary-looking men and women. Were any of them destroyers of public viral ribbon? Appearances could easily deceive in such a forum.

Glad to see you," said a familiar voice. Skopo leaned to his left, where Trepo Lenad stood in the narrow central aisle. The waiter, wearing a bright banana-colored suit, held a thick paper folder under one arm.

"Good evening," smiled Kitanin. "You know Dari here. This is her brother, Mlem. He nodded his head in the direction of the young library aide seated on the opposite side of the female. Dari decided to give an explanation of her brother's presence.

"He and I are eager to improve our health on a carnivorous diet. Already, we see improvement in our body and our stamina."

"I am happy that all of you came," gushed Trepo with a broad grin. "But please excuse me. It is nearly time for me to start proceedings." Bowing, he then hastened to the front of the audience and climbed up on a small stage.

All eyes concentrated on Trepo as he stepped behind a silicon rostrum, placing his folder upon it. He peered out at the assembled listeners.

"I am gratified that so many had the time to come here this evening. Hopefully, you shall learn useful guideposts from my words.

"My topic will be the benefits of increasing the freshness of our meat, milk, and eggs. This is denied by our vegetarian enemies, but let me assure you that they have great numbers. Their attacks upon us never cease.

"The majority on Farmer never taste animal food at all, yet they insist on having fresh vegetables. That is always the crying demand of our neighbors. But ask yourself: don't we deserve to have a fresh animal diet as well?

"Why must our meat be totally imported? Why is the raising of food animals banned on our planet? We want to grow our own supply of flesh for ourselves, but are not permitted to do so.

"That old prohibition is obsolete and must be abolished as soon as possible."

Many enthusiasts in the audience clapped loudly. This rose in volume, becoming general applause. The group of three pretenders joined in with the others as the sound reached its peak.

Trepo glowed with pride, continuing on.

"Raw and lightly cooked meats are full of amino acids and proteins. Animal enzymes enter our stomachs with potency. We receive needed iron that prevents our hemoglobin from falling low in oxygen and causing anemia. We follow the rule: no iron, no oxygen or energy. Only meat guarantees us sufficient iron for good health. That is especially important for females…"

As Trepo droned on, the eyes of Skopo scanned the audience. These were ordinary-looking men and women, nothing particularly noteworthy about them. Yet he saw dedicated fanatics of the animal diet.

How many of them were involved in viral erasing? he wondered.

The speaker continued in a low tone, dreary and monotonous.

"Meat is rich in the mineral of zinc. Our reproductive and immunity systems are dependent upon an adequate supply. Over two hundred enzymes are activated by the zinc we consume. A vegetarian diet risks too low zinc levels."

Skopo speculated whether Trepo was exploiting his father's knowledge of viral science. For what conceivable purpose? Did the carnivore movement have some arcane reason for the senseless destruction of virus memory?

"Are there any questions?" concluded Trepo.

Yes, thought Skopo to himself. Why are you causing harm to the Central Library and our viral communications and memories?

"What is the motive for this evil campaign, and who are your associates?

No one asked the lecturer anything. "Let us now go to the non-vegetarian refreshment table, then," he proposed to all his audience.

* * *

Kitanin and Dari stood before Trepo, eating cheese tidbits.

"You weren't at work today," grinned the detective. "The tall man who served us said that you had to stay home."

Lenad's face blanched white. "My father has been very ill of late," he explained. "I was with him most of the day."

"I hope he feels better soon," smiled Dari with sympathy.

"Thank you," replied the waiter. "Father is now resting at home."

"He is there by himself?" said the investigator with curiosity.

"Yes. Father quieted down sufficiently to allow him to fall asleep."

A bold inquiry then came from Mlem. "What is the nature of his illness?"

Skopo and Dari looked at him with alarm, then turned back to Trepo again.

Had the question unsettled or disturbed their suspect?

"My father worked for years with viral ribbon. His sickness is one of the hazards of constant contact with viruses. He began to suffer toxic infection about two years ago. He has had to quit working ever since becoming bedridden. His condition has become steadily worse."

Vengeance, mused Skopo. The son seeking revenge for what happened to his invalid father.

Trepo pointed to the raw meat sandwiches on the table behind them.

"Those are delicious," said the lecturer. "I think I'll have another one."

As he moved away, Dari and Skopo exchanged brief, meaningful looks.

What now? each of them wondered.

The crowd gathered about the refreshment snacks made way for the evening's speaker. But Trepo suddenly stopped, his eyes catching sight of someone just entering the hall. The waiter turned around and made a dash for the door of the hall.

Skopo, Dari, and Mlem watched, as most of the others did.

Trepo seemed electrified by what he had spied.

A bent, stooped little man with a ghostly bluish face stumbled forward on a polymetal cane. Each step was slow and tentative.

All at once, his legs collapsed before Trepo could reach him. The stricken body fell to the floor helplessly, along with the cane.

Trepo placed his arms around the waist of the desperately panting figure. Several individuals rushed up to help him. Together, they lifted the one who had fainted and carried him to a nearby chair, where they deposited him.

A volunteer went to fetch water. Trepo hovered over the pale-faced oldster.

"Father, why did you come here for?"

The onlookers watched spellbound as the leader lifted the cup for the sick one to drink from.

Skopo, a few feet away, decided to intercede. "Can I see and examine him?" he proposed. "I have had first-aid training and experience." There flashed through his mind images of emergency classes at Kalender Police Academy.

The crowd made room for the detective to approach and feel the forehead of the invalid. He then checked the wrist for the man's pulse.

Skopo turned to the son and spoke in a lowered voice.

"I think he is suffering from exhaustion. It must have taken an enormous effort to walk here. His heart is beating fast and he is running a high fever. His face shows the blue color of viral disease.

"Your father needs immediate rest in order to recover his strength. Can we get him quickly to the nearest hospital?"

The waiter nodded in agreement. "Yes, that would be best."

Mlem spoke up. "I'll go outside and look for a public carrier or taxi."

"A good idea," approved Skopo. "Go at once and find us a motorbox."

People were leaving the meeting hall, perhaps frightened by the blue palour of the viral victim.

Dari bravely took the father's right hand and held it tightly.

"You will be all right," she calmly whispered. "For now, just rest and think of nothing."

"Let me try a head massage," said Skopo from behind her. Dari allowed him to take her place in front of Vrem Lenad.

The detective leaned forward, placed his hands on the latter's head, and slowly applied pressure as he began to make circular motions. In a little while, the viral engineer closed his eyes and fell into slumber.

Meanwhile, Mlem Totmax hailed an empty motorbox. The driver steered the three-wheeled vehicle to the entrance of the meeting hall.

"Stay here till we carry an ailing passenger out of this building," commanded the young man. "Can you drive him to a hospital?"

"Of course," replied the driver. "That would be Kalender Hydroclinic. It is less than a mile from where we now are."

 VIROIDS

Mlem hurried back into the hall and announced he had found a street carrier to take the fallen one to a medical facility.

Skopo helped Trepo lift his sleeping father and carry him outside to the waiting motorbox.

Since the vehicle had only two empty seats, one in front and one behind the driver, there was a problem of how to accompany the patient.

"We will walk to the Hydroclinic, while you ride with your father," Skopo said to Trepo. "See that he immediately receives attention from medicos there."

The motorbox began to roll forward over the smooth cobblestone with father and son inside it.

The three pseudo-carnivores followed on foot.

VII.

Water for every pain or illness. That was the motto of the hydrotherapy that had evolved over many centuries on Farmer. From custom and tradition grew a unique system of treatment and cure. Salt water, alkaloid water, acidic water, ionized water, hydrolyzed water, mineralized water: all had been tried and tested over the generations. All had found their place in the science and art of healing. Physicians used hydraulic immersion in the treatment of most illnesses.

In the forefront of advanced research stood Kalender Hydroclinic. Its tanks and chambers were the best anywhere. Patients came from all sections of Farmer. The reputation of the institution was the highest. Its emergency unit was always busy and packed with people.

Skopo led his companions into the crowded central corridor in the rear of the clinic. Scores of gurneys with newly admitted patients lined the walls. Trepo was first to catch sight of his father, lying under a yellow plastic sheet. He ran to where a nurse was reading the dials of a monitoring device attached to the chest of Vrem.

The four congregated alongside the gurney. Moans and groans rose everywhere in the corridor, but not from the father of Trepo. He was still and silent, with his eyes shut.

The nurse looked up. "He is under sedation," she explained, then walked off.

There was less blueness in Vrem's face, Skopo noticed.

The detective whispered to Trepo. "Has anything like this happened before?"

"Several times, but this is the worst he has ever been," answered the son.

It was at that point that a gigantic male appeared, towering above all four of them. The giant in a brilliant yellow suit had blazing brown eyes in a dark, square face. He exuded an intense inner energy of brain and nerves as he moved past them to the side of the gurney. His right hand felt the left wrist of Vrem as he studied the dials on the monitor unit.

Trepo whispered to his three companions. "This is Dr. Atat, my father's physician."

The latter looked at the group a moment, then spoke to Trepo.

"They paged me by viroidfon as soon as he was brought here. It was a good thing he had his identity band in his wallet, because I was noted there as the medical to call in case of emergency."

"Thank you for arriving so swiftly, sir," softly said the son. Remembering he was not alone there, he introduced the new carnivores to the doctor.

"How serious do you believe this attack was for him?" continued Trepo, anxiety in his voice. "Can anything be done for him here in this clinic?"

The physician lowered his voice to a barely audible murmur.

"Virus has spread through the lymphatic system to all parts of the body. I am going to prescribe a helium flush immediately, as soon as possible."

"Will that save him?" pleaded the son.

"It will take several hours of preparation to have him ready to enter a hydraulic chamber. I think that the pressurized helium can start penetrating through his skin before dawn in the morning."

"Isn't it quite risky?" trembled Trepo.

"There is no other way to attain total detoxification," said the physician. "It will be a highly critical treatment, but it will clean your father of all traces of the virus that is poisoning his body."

The waiter thought a moment. "If there is no alterative to a helium flush…"

"I myself will supervise his immersion," promised Dr. Atat.

At that second, two strong men in green uniform appeared. The group made way so they could wheel away the gurney with Vrem on it.

"I must go with them to oversee what is done," said Atat to the others.

Once he and the gurney were gone, those left in the corridor waited a moment before heading for the entrance to the emergency unit.

The night air was cool and refreshing to the foursome.

As the new carnivores took leave of Trepo, Skopo made sure to get his viroidfon code so he could call and ask about his father's health the next day.

❋ ❋ ❋

Early next morning, Skopo made a report to his immediate superior, Chief of Detectives Yato Pmom. The latter stared at him with unblinking eyes as the events of the previous night were narrated for him.

When Kitanin had finished, the Chief rose from his chair and started pacing about the office. "The erasures are growing more frequent and serious," he grumbled. "Late yesterday afternoon, the target became the Tax Department memory center, wiping out important tax records. All the viroid lines used in reporting and collecting information from businesses and industrial factories are in grave peril. No one can foresee what the vandals might accomplish in the period ahead."

Skopo frowned. "What can we do? Arrest all the carnivores associated with the Lenads? That might not even be enough."

"Is this doctor somehow involved?" asked Pmom, standing in front of the sitting detective and focusing on him.

"I can't say for sure, not yet," replied Skopo.

"Anything on him in our viroid files?"

"Just the basics. This hydrophysician, Predo Atat, is the grandson of the controversial inventor, Zado Atat. He has a brother named for their grandfather. This second Zado Atat operates a language school. The one who practices medicine is an expert in viral poisoning. He has done important research on metallic and mineral toxicity from contact with memory units. His articles have appeared in important medical journals and on viroidline."

"That is interesting, Skopo, but what does it mean? Is this doctor connected to the erasure attacks?"

"I don't want to speculate at present, but he seems to have a reason to seek vengeance for what happened to his grandfather years ago."

"Revenge for insults and attacks two generations ago?" countered the Chief.

"Anything is possible when a family feels that wrong was done to it. Both this doctor and his brother from the language school may be harboring old grudges against viroid makers and users. I intend to investigate both brothers."

"Be careful," warned Pmom. "It may be dangerous ground around these two."

VIII.

The papex sign over the entrance to the Central Library proclaimed its message in stark, large letters. "Closed Until Further Notice".

Kitanin turned about and headed for the flat occupied by the two Totmaxes.

An excited crowd, watching a huge viral screen mounted over the marquee of a department store, blocked his way forward. It was a news program that mesmerized them. More memory erasures were happening, oftener than ever before.

The vandalism was turning into an unstoppable epidemic.

Within minutes, he was at the apartment building and ascended to where his associates lived.

Mlem opened the door and led him in. "You know about the Library, then?"

"I saw the sign," said Skopo as Dari stepped in from the kitchen.

"Good morning," she wearily smiled. "We are home today, until the library building is again safe for operation. The viroid destruction has to end before that can happen."

"The attacks have spread everywhere. Government, banking, business, industry, schools, theaters. No viroid ribbon is safe anywhere."

All of a sudden, Mlem made an unexpected, unforeseeable proposal.

"Since last night I have been thinking over how I could go to the Atat Language School and enroll in one of their courses. That might be the way to unravel the riddle of the group we are interested in. If Dr. Predo Atat is involved in erasures, then his brother is also probably in with him. Or, at least, Zado knows the extent of the conspiracy. So far, there is no proof of anything beyond Trepo Lenad and his wand. If I could explore this school, we might catch hold of what lies behind all this evil destruction."

Skopo peered at him with skepticism. "Such an attempt requires experience that you have not had, Mlem," he murmured soothingly. "You would be taking great risk. Do you know what you will be looking for in this school?"

"I will go along with you," volunteered Dari. "Two agents can do more than just one."

"I don't want the two of you to take on such a dangerous assignment on your own," forcefully asserted the detective. "There is one way of protecting both of you."

"What is that?" eagerly inquired Dari.

"The two of you must wear warners that can send signals through walls. I will be hovering about outside with a receiver unit."

"That sounds pretty secure," said Mlem with enthusiasm. "We can start for the school as soon as we have these warners attached to us."

Soon Skopo left for police headquarters to obtain the devices they would be carrying in the next stage of investigation of the viroid attacks.

He smiled as he realized that his partners were still ignorant of his official role in what they were involved in.

VIII.

The building was a blood red silicon structure from the age before the viroid revolution. It was on an undistinguished side street in the artistic quarter of Kalender. Painters, actors, and writers were neighbors of the rundown Atat Language School. Dirty, dusty windows revealed the fallen state of the premises where students studied the many tongues of the planet Farmer.

Less than a quarter mile from the crimson edifice was a small park concealed under the shelter of giant century trees. Here, alone on a polyplastic bench, Skopo sat with a tiny etherwave receiver on his lap. It was tuned to a music frequency, but inside the donut-shaped apparatus was a warner ready to capture any signal sent from the Totaxes should they fall into an awkward situation. The selections from the classical repertoire of Farmer were sweet and melodic, their rhythms slow and unvarying. Just an ordinary citizen with time on his hands, enjoying the shady centuries and old musical favorites.

Meanwhile, his investigative colleagues were visible to him as they walked along the cobblestone, stopped at the blood red building, and entered its great polymetal door.

Both Dari and Mlem felt inner trepidation as they approached a woman sitting at an old, second-hand desk. Her whitish blond hair was piled up in an outdated, country-style bun.

"Yes?" she asked politely. "Can I be of help to you?"

The sister did the talking for the pair.

"We are both interested in learning other languages," she announced in a low, confident voice.

"Have you decided which ones?" sympathetically inquired the woman with the bun.

"Indeed," grinned Dari. "Both of us agree on that. I myself am interested in studying Laftian, while my brother would like to master the Onxsian language. We plan to take a long voyage around Farmer, so it will be necessary for us to begin our studies as soon as possible. There is no time to lose. Could we start our training in these tongues without delay?"

The secretary sprang out of her polyfabric chair. "Are you familiar with the flash viroid method of condensed learning?"

"No," admitted the librarian without embarrassment. "Neither is my brother. But we are both very eager to use whatever system will succeed in cutting to a minimum the time involved in our instruction."

The whitish blond smiled at Dari. "You must meet our director at once, then." She started to move toward a closed door behind her desk. "If you will wait a moment, I can get Mr. Atat to explain everything for you."

She stepped over to the door, opened it, and disappeared into the interior of the school.

The Totmaxes silently glanced at each other. The plan was a success, so far. But what was to happen once they faced the man in charge here?

The secretary returned in less than a minute.

"He can see you at once. Please go through the door there."

Dari moved forward first, followed by Mlem. In seconds, they were in a spacious, airy office with walls of paneled funguswood. There was a strange aura of time long past about the wide room. Behind a high desk of real wainwood stood a tall. bulky male who had many of the features of the physician they had seen at the Hydroclinic the previous evening. That had been Dr. Predo Atat, the viral disease specialist. This was Zado, the linguistic educator and technician.

The most noticeable difference between the siblings was a greater degree of liveliness in the yellowish eyes of Zado, totally absent in his brother.

"Come, sit down," invited the director, nodding toward two chairs of natural bundlewood.

Unlike the voice of his brother, Zado possessed a tinny tenor.

As the would-be students sat down, so did the big man they had to convince to admit them into the language school.

"What are the languages are you specifically interested in?" asked Atat. "We teach all the many tongues spoken today on Farmer."

Dari spoke for both siblings. "Laftian for me, Onxsian for my brother. We must master them as quickly as we can, so that our travel plans can be facilitated. For us, learning to speak and understand these languages is urgent."

"I understand," nodded Zado Atat. "Let me assure you, it can be done if both of you have the will and determination to accomplish it. First of all, are you at all familiar with our flash vibroid ribbon technique?"

"Hardly at all," responded Dari.

"This method is difficult and demanding. It depends on high-speed viral ribbons that immerse the student in a totally foreign environment. The instruction occurs in a special gyroscopic unit that we call the spinner. This apparatus revolves with incredible velocity, creating an enhanced psychological state favorable to language learning and comprehension."

Mlem then spoke. "How soon can we start? We have no time to lose."

"A new group will begin this afternoon at two o'clock. I shall be holding an orientation session for them. If you two wish, my secretary can enroll you in this class of beginners."

"That would be fine," beamed Dari.

"She can handle the fees for you," declared Zado. "If any questions whatsoever come up, do not hesitate to ask me at once."

We will, thought Dari. Indeed, we will.

✦ ✦ ✦

The detective caught sight of his two confederates leaving the language school. He followed them for a short time, then rushed forward to find out what had happened.

"How did it go?"

"Smoothly," replied Dari, walking along slowly.

"Zado Atat was friendly and easy to deal with," added her brother.

"This afternoon at two, we attend an introductory class," continued Dari. "There was no sign of suspicion at all." She went on to describe how the spinning chamber was to be used on them.

Skopo thought a second. "The two of you should return to your flat and rest up for what is to come. I myself will go to the Carnavan and see Trepo."

"You will find out how his father is recovering?" said the librarian.

"Precisely. I can buy some sandwiches for the three of us and then come to your apartment."

Dari smiled. "Mlem and I will be expecting you, then."

❋ ❋ ❋

As Skopo went to the take-out counter at the Carnavan, he sighted Trepo waving at him from a distance. It took him only seconds to order blood-and-tongue sandwiches for himself and the Totmaxes. He picked up the papex sack containing his purchases, then moved across the room to where Trepo was standing, waiting to be summoned by the next customer to enter the place.

"How are you holding up?" asked Skopo. "Did you get any sleep at all?"

"Only a little," answered the waiter, bags of exhaustion under his eyes.

"How is your father's condition? Do you know?"

"Dr. Atat was there when they placed him in the hydraulic chamber for heliumization. The plan is to take him out this afternoon, at three."

"Are you going to be there for that?"

"Yes, I am taking off from work in order to be present there."

Skopo decided to interpose himself. "If you wish, I can accompany you to the Hydroclinic."

Trepo nodded yes. "I would appreciate not being by myself there."

The other said good-bye, leaving with the takeout sack of sandwiches.

As he hurried toward the Totmax flat, his mind reviewed the situation, considering the connections between different parts and aspects.

Dari and Mlem were watching and listening to news on the viroid tube in their living room.

"Let's go into the kitchen unit and eat," suggested Dari, rising from her chair and turning off the picture set from the control band on the armrest.

"A lot of bad news," muttered Mlem as the three went into the back room. "More vandalism reported. All the major banks have been victims. So have many factories. Schools in Kalender are closing. Normal patterns of life have all been ended as long as this continues."

The trio sat down at a small circular table and began to consume the blood-and-tongue sandwiches. Mlem obtained a jug of vegetable juice from the freeze unit.

As they went at the food, Dari chuckled to herself. The other two stared at her.

"I was thinking that if we continue to impersonate animalists, we may end up as used to it that we become habitual, addicted carnivores."

Skopo laughed, but then spoke seriously. "You two must be careful. I have been thinking over the situation at the language school and now suspect that something similar may be going on there."

The Totmaxes waited for the inspector to explain.

"Up to now, I supposed that the meat-eaters might be the population from which the vandals might have been recruited. But I observed them at the restaurant, then at the lecture last night. They

     VIROIDS

appeared to be average, everyday people, not too different from everyone else. There were no dangerous signs about them.

"When you told me about the spinner gyroscopes that Zado Atat uses in language teaching, Dari, it made me think hard. Perhaps there is something else going on, a hidden recruitment and indoctrination."

"You suspect that the readers who destroy viroid memory come from the Atat Language School?" exclaimed the librarian with excitement.

"That is what they may be concealing there. Think of who is involved. Zado Atat, with a grudge against the entire viroid system. Vnem Lenad, a skilled engineer, whose son has destroyed valuable memory at the Central Library." The police officer paused a moment. "You must send me a signal with the warners at the first sign that anyone becomes aware of what you are up to at the school."

IX.

The conference room held fifty or more plastic chairs, half of them filled with new language students.

Dari and Mlem sat beside each other in the second row, in the middle of a group of eager would-be linguists. Most looked very young, realized the two probers.

As they waited for the director to enter, no one in the audience spoke to anyone else.

At last, Zado Atat came in wearing a peppermint-striped suit. He stepped behind a polysteel lectern and began to address the new students in his high tenor voice.

"Welcome to the Atat School, dear students.

"Often people believe this institution is named for its present director, who is now addressing you. That, though, is not the case. The person who is thus honored happens to have been my late grandfather, Zado Atat, for whom I was named.

"You may have heard of him in connection with his pioneering work in the development of viroid memory. In actual fact, he was the true inventor of the ribbon that revolutionized communications and data storage on our planet. Nothing would be as it is today were it not for his seminal discoveries. When the history of that era is finally written in accurate detail, all of Farmer will acknowledge his greatness as a scientist. The future, I predict, will rectify the mistaken version of what occurred. The official interpretations will crumble and disappear.

"Let me assure you that the method of language instruction we use here is an advanced application of the principles created by my grandfather. Our instructional ribbons flash by on a projection screen at a high speed that is regulated by the individual student. Our specially designed and engineered learning sphere spins about at a rate that induces the optimal reception state in a student. You will all receive training in the operation of the gyroscopic chamber and the projected viroid ribbons. The learning rate of your chosen language will be completely up to you.

"Think of it. The images emitted by the viroid device will take up the entire inside surface of the sphere. You will have control over the speed of the spin, and of the vertical and horizontal positioning of the unit. All of the many parameters are instantly changeable in order to serve the needs of the individual learner.

"The spin chamber places a student into a properly suitable state of mind for efficient mastery of a language. Learning becomes instant and immediate. Within minutes, the person answers questions and can speak in the new tongue. Total immersion in the lingual atmosphere is the result. Within days, mastery is attained.

"Have no fear of the gyrating sphere you will be in. It is perfectly safe. There has never been any accident or injury. Hundreds of people have been trained with our viroid ribbons. The structural matrix and lexical fund of each language system is transferred into the mind through eye, ear, and touch. Your very nerves will learn a new code. The details will fall into place and become clear as you go forward."

Zado Atat stopped, drew a deep breath, then peered out at his spellbound audience.

"Does anyone have any questions about what lies ahead?" he asked in a muffled tone.

For several seconds, the conference room was without sound of any sort. Then, a young man in the last row raised a hand and spoke.

"I was wondering, sir, how long this period of initial adjustment to the full spinning speed will last."

"It all depends," replied the director, pleasantly smiling. "For some, the process is short and quick. Others may have to take a longer time in order to become acquainted with the operation of the gyroscopic controls and the motion of the viroid ribbons."

"Thank you, sir," meekly said the questioner.

As soon as he sat down, a squat middle-aged matron in front of Mlem leaped up and asked Atat how good a mastery of her chosen language she would enjoy.

The director gazed at her benignly with a warm grin.

"Better than that of the average native," he informed her. "That is how sharp your ability will be. Everyone will marvel at you. The results will be astonishing."

Zado scanned across the room. "Any other question?" he muttered, not expecting any more.

Out of the blue, Mlem sprang to his feet.

Dari gave a slight start. What was her brother about to say? Would he compromise their mission here?

"I have heard a lot about viral infection and poisoning," he unexpectedly declared. "Is there any danger of accidental exposure to toxic organisms inside the gyrosphere? Has anyone at this school ever suffered an illness of any kind?"

Zado's eyes turned into burning coals. His face flooded with blood. For a brief moment, he was at a loss for the right words with which to handle the situation.

"No," he blurted with finality. "We have always kept within the boundaries of viral safety. Our technical staff takes all necessary precautions to protect our students."

Mlem sat down without thanking him for the answer. He glanced for a second at his sister out of the corner of his eye. Both of them realized that they had just heard a lie from the head of the school.

Zado Atat ended the introductory session with a curt dismissal of the group.

❊ ❊ ❊

It was late afternoon when the Totmaxes emerged from the blood red building.

Skopo Kitanin shut off his etherwave receiver and rose from the park bench he had been occupying while the others had been within the language school.

Strolling briskly along with the receiver hanging from his pants belt, he caught up with the pair.

Dari began talking as soon as the detective reached them.

"We climbed into two of the gyrospheres and learned how to operate the controls. But we shall not begin to spin until this evening. That's when the language ribbons will be inserted and run through. Mlem and I will be in the first group scheduled for actual instruction."

The threesome walked forward at a leisurely pace.

"What was Zado Atat like?" asked Skopo. "How did he treat the students?"

Mlem was the one who answered. "To me, he appeared to be making a phony, exaggerated effort to be warm and hospitable, as if he was trying to convince them they should trust him completely."

"The director was much more personal toward the two of us later than when we introduced ourselves in his office this morning," noted Dari.

"Did he ask you what you did for a living?"

"No. He took us at face value as travelers with urgent linguistic needs. But I noticed that he was very interested in the extent of our technical knowledge and experience with viroid ribbons. And the same was true for the other students in the group, as far as I could tell." Dari suddenly remembered something. "He mentioned the school's viral engineer in passing, but not by name."

"What did Zado say about him?" eagerly asked Skopo, his eyes turned toward the librarian.

"Nothing much, except that he was away on sudden, emergency leave."

The investigator scowled darkly. "Trepo reported that his father is still recovering from his treatment in the helium chamber. He will, in all probability, be returning to some semblance of consciousness this evening. What he reveals in the first flush of awakening could be unusually candid. His guard will be down for a short period of time."

Dari looked at him from the corner of her eye. "What do you plan to do, Skopo?"

All of a sudden, the latter stopped in his tracks. Dari, then Mlem, did likewise.

"I want both of you to go back to your apartment and wait for me there. We can talk again before you return to the school tonight."

Dari looked alarmed. "You are going to see the father of Trepo at the Hydroclinic?" she inquired.

"Precisely." Skopo removed the etherwave receiver from his belt and handed it to Mlem.

Then he took his leave and headed in a different direction, toward the Hydroclinic and the old man recovering from immersion in helium-saturated water.

X.

Each separate cell of the recovery section contained a flotation bed resting in a tank of specially aerated fluid.

Skopo found it quite easy to enter this area within the Hydroclinic inhindered and undetected. But in which of the cubicles within the complicated hive was he to look for the father of Trepo Lenad?

He stood in the narrow corridor, pondering what to do next, when a nurse in red uniform came up to him from behind. "Can I help you, sir?" she asked.

Without turning about, the intruder answered curtly. "I can't find a patient whom I came to have a look at. He is Vnem Lenad, the viral poisoning victim."

Not seeing his face, the woman gave him simple directions. "That person is in the next-to-the-last cell on the left side, close to the end."

"Thank you."

Skopo made his way to where she had instructed him to go. A polyplastic curtain covered the entrance to the tiny cubicle enclosed within silicon walls.

The detective parted the two halves and tiptoes into the darkened alcove. He could make out the lower end of the undulating floater upon which rested the body of the one in recovery. The polyfabric bed, resting on a boatlike frame, made continual little movements up-and-down. As his eyes became accustomed to the dimness, Skopo identified the outline of the viroid engineer below at the level of the cell's floor.

He moved toward the flotation bed slowly and cautiously. Only when a foot away from the lying patient did a sudden realization come to him.

The man on the surface of the liquid was wide awake.

A mumbling sound arose from the center of the cubicle. Vnem Lenad was whispering something in a trancelike state just below awakened consciousness.

"Trepo…Trepo…" sounded from the rasping throat.

The unauthorized visitor moved closer to the edge of the floating bed. He dared not say anything, though it was clear that the patient, even in half-sleep, sensed the presence of another, taking him for the son he was calling to.

"Trepo, tell them there is grave danger in the sphere."

The words were very low, but audible. A warning about the viral poisoning that had infected him, meant for the son he believed present in the cubicle.

Skopo wished for more, but nothing came from the stricken engineer.

All at once, he heard a slight sound of movement. The polyplastic curtain over the entrance rustled, indicating a new presence.

The investigator swiveled himself about.

A bulky, threatening shape formed at the boundary of the corridor, staring into the cell.

It took Skopo less than an instant to identify the hydraulic physician, Dr. Predo Atat.

❀ ❀ ❀

A familiar voice sounded, but it did not come from the towering man standing in the entrance to the recovery cubicle.

"It is good of you to have come here, gradually whispered Trepo Lenad.

Immediately behind the doctor is the waiter, the relieved detective told himself.

Predo Atat stepped a few inches to the side, making visible the presence of the patient's son. A careful movement occurred as Skopo slipped past the bulking figure, making his exit from the cell where Vnem Lenad still slept.

Atat turned around so that he could see both of the visitors.

"I arrived a moment ago," explained Skopo. "Your father remains in a sleeping trance, Trepo."

The latter looked over the investigator's right shoulder, into the face of the hydrophysician.

"Should he not have awakened by now?" said the troubled son.

"In most cases, yes. But your father was an extreme example of toxicity. I had to keep him in the hydrochamber for several hours beyond the normal treatment period. That is the reason he has not yet reached consciousness. But I expect that his awakening is very near. It won't occur any later than the next hour or so, I estimate."

Skopo made an instant decision to address Trepo with a proposal.

"I could stay here with you so that you wouldn't be alone," he told the waiter.

"That will not be necessary," replied Predo Atat instead of the one being spoken to. "I myself am off-duty at the moment, so that the two of us can be in this cubicle when the awakening comes about." The gigantic doctor pursed his mouth. "It is best if you return tomorrow morning," he said to Skopo.

The detective gave a nod to Atat, then another to Trepo before exiting into the corridor.

It was time for him to think about what he had heard the patient mumble in his sleep.

XII.

As they walked toward the language school, the police detective related to Dari and Mlem what he had witnessed and heard in the flotation cubicle at the Hydroclinic.

"I want you both to be extremely careful," he cautioned them. "Don't take chances that could expose why you are there at the school."

Dari made a reply. "We'll try to learn all we can without acting suspiciously."

"I'll look out for my sister," promised Mlem. "If anything should happen, we both have warners you can pick up from a distance outside."

Skopo said good-bye to the Totmaxes, heading for the park where he planned to sit and listen to his etherwave receiver.

Dari and her brother arrived early at the blood red building. Finding no one at the reception desk in the front lobby of the school, they saw their chance to look around before the evening contingent of students.

The two siblings exchanged glances. They were in tacit agreement on seeing the opportunity provided them by the situation. Without making the slightest noise, brother and sister made their way slowly down the main corridor, to a large orange-colored door made of polymetal. A sign with luminescent letters spelled out a single word: "Spheres".

They stopped and turned to each other. Dari was the one to suggest "Let's go in." She whispered it under her breath.

Mlem opened it carefully. No one appeared to be about. It was a long, large room. Dari slipped inside as he held it open for her. Then he followed her in, letting the door slide shut.

A line of twelve round gyrospheres stood on the left side of the spacious hall where instruction went on. In front of each device there

　　　　　VIROIDS

was a control console with tabs, switches, buttons, and dials. Only one of the spheres was in operation, spinning rapidly on a bed of magnetically ionized compressed air. A low, steady hum was clearly audible.

The Totmaxes moved forward, toward the whirling spherical cabin suspended inches above the concave silicon flooring on which it rested when not in motion.

The rotating polymetal globe touched nothing but pressurized air.

Above, below, and on all sides there was perfect transparency. From the silicon bed under the sphere rose the submagnetic force producing the spin of the mechanism.

All eleven of the other cabins rested securely on their separate bases, the indented circles matching the bottom one-eighth of each of the spheres.

Suddenly, the sound of a door opening reached the ears of the sister and brother. Both of them whirled around to see who it was.

A rotund little man was walking directly toward them. He wore a straw-colored coat of natural papex. His hair and bushy moustache were dark hudnut brown.

Who could this be? wondered the librarian and her brother.

The newcomer was a few feet away when he started to speak.

"You must be new students," he drawled out of the corner of his mouth.

"That's correct," responded Dari with a forced smile. "We came a bit early for our first instructional session. That is set for this evening."

She and Mlem waited to see what the stranger's reaction would be.

"Let me introduce myself. My name is Frango Barut, but everyone here at the school calls me Frango the Polyglot. That is because I have succeeded in gaining fluency in fifteen foreign languages up to now. I am, at the present time, preparing to master my sixteenth." His brown eyes grew darker and larger. "A person can never know too many tongues, isn't that true? My ambition is to set a record for the entire planet of Farmer. I have only ten more to go in order to reach that goal."

Dari grinned at the round little man. "You must have spent a lot of time inside the gyrospheres," she made herself say with admiration.

Frango smiled from ear-to-ear with pride. His circular face reddened. "What languages do the two of you plan to study?" he asked.

"I have chosen Laftian," said Dari. "My brother intends to master Onxsian. Are either of those among the fifteen you've learned?"

The polyglot beamed at both of them. "Indeed, both of them are beautiful, as well as useful. I know them quite well, and can give you suggestions on some of their fine points."

"We would be very grateful for that," smiled the sister.

"I try to come here whenever my business allows me to. But my restaurant demands my attention almost all day long. Perhaps you have heard of it. The name is the Carnavan. It caters to the needs of animal-eaters."

The Totmaxes stifled their inner surprise. Neither coughed, choked, or showed emotional effect.

What could they say? Dari glanced for an instant at her brother, then addressed the short, fat man with the unusual connection.

"We have eaten there with carnivore friends," she noted nonchalantly. "The food served is delightful."

Frango went on. "I myself am only a partial carnivore. Most of the time, I am only an old-fashioned vegetarian. My main reason for opening the restaurant was, frankly, a simple economic one. I thought that I could make a good living for myself, and that proved to be true. The business takes up very little of my day, so that I can devote a lot of time to my main love, linguistics."

"How convenient!" sighed Dari.

"In fact, many of the students at the school have become carnivores and now regularly frequent my establishment."

"You convince them to try the animal diet?" inquired Mlem.

　　　　　　　VIROIDS

The fat man's moustache twisted a little. "Not intentionally. I merely inform them about the kind of restaurant I run. They come there on their own."

"That's interesting," murmured Dari. "Are the personnel of the school also frequent customers at your place?"

"Yes, indeed. The chief engineer who supervises the spheres here has a son who works as a waiter at the Carnavan." A dark cloud seemed to fall over the face of the polyglot. "The father is not well. I understand he has been hospitalized."

"That's too bad," continued the librarian. "I hope it's nothing serious."

Frango appeared troubled, hesitating before he went on.

"A touch of viral poison," he sadly muttered. "It is hoped he will return to the school before too long."

At that moment, the entrance to the long room opened. Zado Atat lumbered in, spotting the group of three students and approaching them.

"Good evening," he called out. "You are here early."

"I've introduced myself," said Frango. "These new students are eager to study and learn."

"Let's get started, then." Atat moved closer to them. "Since you three are here first, you can take Sphere One, Two, and Three." He pointed toward the upper end of the row of gyrospheres. "I myself will load the ribbons into the viewer boxes. Our chief technician is not present to supervise tonight."

"Is he still in the hospital?" asked the polyglot.

"It will be a long time before Vnem is able to return to us," solemnly noted the director.

The Totmaxes prepared to enter the learning spheres assigned them.

✦ ✦ ✦

Although Dari and Mlem were going to study different languages, their ribbons began with the same introductory section. This methodological preface was meant to place the student into a passive, receptive state of mind.

"In order to get the most out of your instruction experience, you must put everything else out of your mind. That is the reason for being inside the spinning gyrosphere. The flash ribbon, as you now can see, is being projected onto the screen that envelopes you completely. The lingual environment will be above, below, and about you in every direction. The result is total saturation. But your own attitude will be the main ingredient for successful learning on your part.

"Try to be relaxed and at ease. Do not focus on any single portion of the scene on the surrounding screen, but take it in as a whole. Let the outside world drift away. Listen attentively to every word that you hear spoken. Forget all daily cares and worries. Your attention must center, without any exception, upon what sight, sound, or touch offer and present before you.

"Rest, let go, and submit to the immediate environment inside the sphere. Surrender your will to the viroid ribbon images all about you. They are the only reality left. Nothing else matters. Remember: you must relax, let go, and submit. Do not let any obstacle, even your own will, stand in the way of learning the language. Success is guaranteed when cooperation occurs. The greater your compliance with these directions, the easier will be the course of your instruction.

"Now, repeat the central formula of linguistic mastery after me: rest, let go, submit. Rest, let go, submit. Rest, let go, submit…"

In less than a minute, the Totmaxes were engaged in committing to memory the basic pronouns and prepositions of their respective languages. I, you, he, she, it. We, you, they. At, by, in, on, over, with, etc. Within the first five minutes, all this was to be mastered.

Soon after that, physical objects began to appear on the viroid screen. Simultaneously, the name of the noun became audible, as well as written out in large letters under the image of the particular item.

At the rate of one word per second, a vocabulary of six hundred words was learned within the period lasting ten minutes.

The next fifteen minutes were devoted to sentence formation with verb forms. Conjugation of verbs sunk into the brain. A question-and-answer format was applied, with the viroid ribbon acting as the instructor, grilling the student. What is this? What is this person doing? Describe this scene.

At the end of half an hour, both Dari and Mlem were in conversation with their respective ribbon systems. Twenty minutes of this rapid speed give-and-take, and each of them had acquired a fundamental knowledge of either Laftian or Onxsian.

When the fifty minute session ended, the gyrospheres started to slow down, finally stopping their spinning. The viroid screens were all at once devoid of images. As if awakening from an eerie dream, both Totmaxes felt exhilarated and refreshed.

Zado Atat opened the hatch of Dari's sphere and helped her out. Amazingly, she sensed no dizziness whatever. Next, the director did the same for her brother.

Excited and enraptured, Dari asked him when they could return for their next session in the spheres.

Atat grinned foxily at the librarian. "That will be for the intermediate viroid ribbons, won't it? I believe that there will be two gyrospheres available for you and your brother early tomorrow morning. Can the two of you be here at eight?"

Dari and Mlem assured him they could, then hurried out of the Atat Language School as soon as seemed adequate to maintain their cover as ordinary travelers learning new languages.

There was a lot that Skopo would be glad to hear about their experiences in the spinning globes, as well as the new acquaintance they had made with the restaurant-owner who had become a polyglot at the language school.

XIII.

The walk back to the Totmax apartment was taken up with vigorous exchange.

Both Dari and Mlem described the experience both had before and during the spinning of the units they were in.

"The viroid ribbons were mesmeric and intense," held the librarian. "They captured you to the bottom of your psyche and being." She breathed out a lengthy sigh.

As he strolled along beside the two, the detective considered the options lying ahead for them. What was the best course to a non-violent, non-lethal solution? How could the expanding viroid vandalism be stopped both speedily and safely?

Skopo suddenly stopped, then his companions did the same.

"I want you both to get a good night's sleep," he told them. "Tomorrow will present some possible difficulties when you return to the school. I'll be back to see you two early in the morning."

Dari gave him a worried look. "What are you planning to do until then?"

The investigator made a mysterious grin. "I'm not certain yet, to tell the truth. My first task will be to have contact with my boss at police headquarters. I am an official government investigator, not at all working on my own as a private agent. My work with you is serious and professional."

"Will your chief be there at this hour?" said the librarian with surprise.

"He's always there, except for a few hours off."

Skopo gave a little nod, then turned and rushed away.

❖ ❖ ❖

Yato Pmom's face was ashen as the detective gave him a concise but accurate report.

After it finished, neither police officer spoke for a considerable time. The silence was broken, at last, by Skopo.

"The time to move in on them may soon be here," he thoughtfully said. "We know that both the Carnavan Restaurant and the Atat school are involved in this strange, evil conspiracy."

Pmom pondered intensely several seconds. He slumped lower in his desk chair.

"I will have both locations surrounded a little before dawn," answered the chief. "My men must be ready to move in at the first signal from me."

"And when will you give that?" anxiously inquired Skopo.

Yato Pmom looked away. "That remains to be decided," he grumbled. "Your friends intend to return for further instruction tomorrow?"

"Yes. But I fear for their safety. Perhaps we should call their mission off."

"Do whatever you think is wisest concerning them, Skopo," advised the superior. "I have total confidence in your judgment."

"Thank you," whispered the detective, rising from his chair.

He already had in mind what he was going to try to accomplish that night.

✦ ✦ ✦

Bad news flashed on viroid screens on street units around the Hydroclinic.

Long-distance viroid cables are suffering memory erasures. Stock and bond markets have been seriously attacked. The sport network no longer functions. All commodity trading is suspended for the foreseeable future. Vandals have cut police viroid data lines. No one and nothing is safe and secure.

Skopo remembered which side corridors to follow in the hospital to avoid most of the medical personnel. He slowed his steps as he approached the recovery section where he had last seen Vrem Lenad. The engineer must still be there in a flotation cell. Would he be willing to reveal any secrets to a stranger he had seen only once before, in the emergency sector of the hospital?

Trepo had introduced him as a fellow carnivore. Perhaps the viroid technician might accept him as one of the vandal conspiracy of criminal readers. That's what Vrem had called his comrades in semi-sleep the previous time he had visited here. They were library readers who performed evil actions.

The detective crept along the narrow way to the floating chambers. Approaching nearer, he heard muffled voices from inside the particular cubicle that he was interested in. Was his plan to talk to Vrem foiled somehow? he wondered with alarm.

Inches from the covered entrance, two distinguishable voices became identifiable. Trepo Lenad was inside the cubicle, conversing with his father.

Stifling his breath, Skopo listened attentively. Words began to combine into coherent phrases and entire sentences.

"This cannot go on," said the gravely voice of the engineer. "There is great danger to you, Trepo. In fact, every single one of the readers may soon become seriously infected. Their wands contain toxic quantities of submagnetic virophaic compounds within many of the viroid ribbons being used."

"We are attempting to correct them, father," announced the voice of the waiter. "But our campaign is in full swing and cannot be stopped at this time."

"Lives are at stake," angrily responded the patient. "I myself came close to death by viroid poisoning. Every single wand must be inspected and sanitized. There is no alternative, if disaster is to be avoided. Where are they now, still stored at the Carnavan? These wands are a danger to anyone who handles them for any long period of time."

     VIROIDS

"Yes. When the restaurant opens tomorrow morning for breakfast, the readers will start reporting there for the wands. All of them are in the viroid chargers, being prepared for future work."

"That is the probable point of contamination, son," weakly croaked Vnem. "Do not let the readers take out any wands without first checking them for virophaics in the viroid streams."

Trepo argued back. "We can't stop what has begun. Every day the school produces new operatives ready to apply what they've learned about memory sabotage. It's grown too big. The time is much too late for any major correction. All we can do is look out for signs of possible poisoning."

"There will be casualties, plenty of them," ominously warned the father.

"That cannot be avoided," countered Trepo. "We knew the risks in this when we started."

Skopo sensed some sort of movement from behind him. He was about to turn around when a powerful blow struck him on the head. Blackness descended upon his eyes and filled his brain, so that the detective became totally unaware of what happened to him next.

Dr. Predo Atat, a heavy piece of polymetal in his right hand, peered down at the crumbled body of the man he had taken for a carnivore friend of the waiter who was the son of this patient of his.

Trepo himself, hearing a sudden noise of something falling, opened the curtain of the cubicle and surveyed the strange situation on the outside.

"I believe we have some sort of spy among us," whispered the hydrophysician.

Trepo and Predo gazed intently at the unconscious man on the floor.

"He was eavesdropping on what you were saying with your father," reported Atat, looking directly at Trepo.

"What do you plan to do with this fellow on the floor?" asked the waiter in a quivering, fearful voice.

"I believe that I know where we can securely store him, till he awakens," the doctor informed him.

XIV.

Skopo could feel the hard polymetal surface of a hospital gurney beneath his prone body. Several straps held him in a rigid, inescapable position. His brain throbbed with a distant pain as he tried to take in the surrounding room. The walls and ceiling were an immaculate white, indicating he was still somewhere within the Hydroclinic.

A door opened and two sets of feet entered the place he was being held in. It took him a while to recognize, from a low angle, the faces of Dr. Predo Atat and Trepo Lenad as they stood on opposite sides of the gurney. He bit his lower lip in stern determination to maintain secrecy, regardless of what might be done to him.

The hydrophysician was the one in charge of the attempted grilling.

"What was your purpose in coming to the Carnavan?"

"Why were you lurking outside the flotation cubicle?"

"How much have you learned about the activities being carried out by our readers?"

"Are you connected with the police in any way?"

The detective maintained a face of flint, not moving a muscle. His training and experience had prepared him for just such a situation as he was now in. Be stubborn, but stay limp, in command of both body and mind. Not a twitch of movement that could signify anything. Pretend that you don't hear the questions being posed. Imagine being elsewhere, in a normal, ordinary surrounding. Far away from here, with someone whose company it is a pleasure to share.

Skopo suddenly thought of Dari Totmax, the librarian awaiting him in this present case of his. Where was she at this hour? What was she involved in?

He realized that he had no knowledge of what time it was after his period of imposed unconsciousness. It might still be night, but day may have already arrived as well. Dari and Mlem would be worried by his absence. What if they decided to stay away from the Atat Language School? They had to have realized that something had gone wrong, that all their plans had to be changed at once.

Do not go to the blood red building, Dari, Skopo wished. Stay out of the spinning learning spheres. The dangers are enormous ones there.

He no longer heard the threatening voice of Predo Atat.

All at once, the gurney he was on began to move.

His captors were going to take him elsewhere.

❋ ❋ ❋

Breakfast was short and quick for the Totmaxes. They left the kitchen and went into the living room to wait for Skopo to arrive.

Time passed at first rapidly, then slowly and anxiously.

Dari looked at her brother at intervals as they sat in expectation of their associate's arrival. Neither voiced the worry each of them felt.

The timer on the wall eventually indicated that they had just enough time left to get to the language school for the scheduled session of instruction inside the gyrospheres.

It was the sister who rose to her feet and said what was in both their minds.

"Something has caused Skopo to be late, but we can't change the plan that was made and that we agreed to. It is up to us now to carry out what all three of us decided."

Mlem sprang up without a word. In a short time, the two were on their way.

Neither of them expressed the inner worry centered over what might have happened to their comrade. Each still carried the warner that was supposed to summon Skopo in case of threat or danger.

They hurried in silence through the now crowded pedestrian side streets of central Kalender. Both looked straight ahead, never glancing at the public viroid news screens at corners along the way. Overnight, governmental archives and statistical collections had become targets of erasure raids. Several departments found themselves seriously crippled by invisible attacks.

Dari and Mlem turned into the side street where the language school was located.

All of a sudden, the brother took his sister's hand and squeezed it tightly.

Then, they broke apart and bravely entered the front door of the crimson silicon structure.

✻ ✻ ✻

Frango the Polyglot was the only person visible in the hall of spheres.

"Good morning, friends," he greeted the new arrivals. "So good to see you here so bright and early."

Only one of the twelve gyrospheres was already in motion, the one at the far end, a distance from the door to the long room.

"We are both scheduled for our intermediate lessons as soon as we settle into two of the spheres," announced Dari. "It is a surprise to see you here so early, Frango."

The latter smiled broadly, but then grimaced. "I expected to come in and jump into my old favorite, at the head of the line." He nodded his head toward the spinning globe at the far end. "It appears, though, that someone got here before me and occupied it before I could."

Mlem tried to console him. "There are all the others that are still not taken. I am sure that they are not all reserved so early in the day."

At that moment, two young language students entered the hall and began to climb into two of the vacant spheres.

"Once a person starts with a particular unit," continued Frango, "it is difficult to change over to another one. For me, the move is almost impossible. That is why I intend to wait until whoever is using my accustomed one finishes. I can't even think of climbing into some other one. That is the only spinner that I feel at home in.

"Wait and see, it will be the same for you."

The restaurant owner pointed to a large canister of viroid ribbons lying on a small silicon table. "I am ready to begin, as soon as my old favorite is available. Do you have the ribbons that you will need this morning?"

"No," answered Dari. "Mr. Atat did all the ribbon loading for us yesterday. We haven't seen him yet today. We don't have the ones we will be using."

"He may be in his office," noted Frango. "If you wish, I could go to the storage chamber and obtain the ones you will be using. Have you had any instruction on how to load the internal projector?"

"No," said Mlem. "We never reached that point, being beginners. I believe that will come up today, at the intermediate level."

"Let me see, you two will be on the second stage level for Laftian and Onxikian. Am I right?"

"Yes," nodded Dari. "But we do not wish to trouble you. We can wait until Mr. Atat is here with us."

"I'll show you how to load up the projection device," offered Frango. By now, two more gyrospheres were in rotation. The one at the far end was spinning furiously at breakneck speed.

As the polyglot made his way toward the supply room, the Totmaxes had their attention drawn to the unusually high whine from the occupied gyro farthest away. Something told them it had reached a dangerous rate of speed. A screeching noise indicated that the sphere had not been built for such rapid acceleration of motion.

Frango, sensing that disaster threatened, walked toward the control board of that particular globe. What was wrong? he wondered, checking the tabs and dials.

Mlem started to move forward, followed by his sister. Their alarm increased by the second. There was no question that this gyrosphere had spun out of control and was nearing the boundary of catastrophe.

Although Frango pushed and pulled at the levers and knobs, this had no effect. The madly whirling sphere made a terrible noise, weird and unworldly. Was the globe about to escape from the enveloping ionized gas, flying off or apart?

"It won't slow down at all," shouted the polyglot, desperately attempting to restore control. "Something horrible may now happen!"

The Totmaxes looked at each other with apprehension. Neither of them could make sense out of the impending disastrous event.

"Where is Mr. Atat?" gaped Mlem. "Why is he not here?"

At that precise moment, the director rushed into the hall. The loud noise of scraping polymetal had reached him in his office in the front.

Zado ran to the control board in question, jostling Frango to one side. He seemed to recognize instantly where the cause of the problem was, crying out two words: "audible contact!"

As soon as he attained that objective through manipulation of the multiple controls, the director began to speak into a tiny transmitter box at the top of the control board.

"Stop this interference," he yelled out. "Slow down and stop, or else the sphere will crash, collapse, and kill you."

Everyone waited to see what would happen next. Dari and Mlem glanced at each other for a second. The swirling globe started to reverse its speed. The scratching and screeching subsided and disappeared as normal rotation was restored.

Slower and slower moved the sphere, till it settled down into its groove. The ionized layer of compressed air vanished. Spinning came to a complete stop.

Zado ran to the hatch and forced it open. A popping noise issued and rushed out of the globe.

Dari moved forward to catch sight of the wayward student who had been inside the chamber. She waited breathlessly to see who had been inside it.

Upon seeing a head emerge through the opening, the librarian came close to falling faint.

Instantly, she pulled herself together and reached under her outer garment to where the tiny alarm sender was attached. She had to try sending a warning signal in hope of someone coming to their rescue.

For it was Skopo Kitanin who had been imprisoned inside the wildly whirling gyroscope.

XV.

It was fortunate that Zado Atat did not realize why the man he had placed in the sphere the previous night was staring so intensely at his newest female language student. Skopo seemed entranced upon catching sight of Dari.

You were here as I tried my last desperate attempt at escape, the detective meditated to himself. After loosening the plastex rope holding me, I tried every possible maneuver I could think of inside this chamber. I had to draw attention on the outside to my grave situation. The flashing of viroid images onto the walls surrounding me came to a stop through my wild motions. I had to act like a mad man in order to put an end to the torture I was suffering inside this globe.

By this time, Trepo had entered and was attempting to help the director lift the limp body of Skopo out of the gyrosphere.

Frango and the Totmaxes stepped out of the way of Zado and Trepo. Dari and Mlem exchanged meaningful looks.

What were they to say or do under the circumstances? How did Skopo come to be imprisoned inside a spinning sphere in the language school?

The two understood it was best that they maintain their charade as language learners. They had to avoid raising any suspicions about why they were present.

Zado gave Trepo a commanding look. "Let's carry him into my office," he ordered out of the corner of his mouth.

But the perplexed waiter failed to move at once. He was staring at Dari.

She was the woman who had eaten at the Carnavan with the traitor, who had attended his lecture on carnivorism in the company of the perfidious infiltrator. She was here at the language school as a student, along with the young man she called her brother.

Trepo reached into his coat pocket and pulled out a tiny micropulser, pointing it at the two Totmaxes.

"I know these two," he informed the director. "They are confederates of the spy we caught."

Atat studied the two students who had just been unmasked as pretenders.

"Take all of them to my office," he commanded the waiter with the weapon.

Frango intervened. "What is going on here? I don't understand why all this is happening. It makes no sense at all to me."

"These people are dangerous criminals," muttered the director. "I will explain all of this to you later, Frango."

Skopo listened to these exchanges while still sitting inside the sphere, gathering his strength and restoring some measure of balance to himself.

He started to rise and emerge out of the hatch on his own. Steadying himself, he stepped out onto the floor of the hall.

Trepo extended an arm, grabbing hold of the detective's pants belt and pointing his micropulser at him.

"Come with me," he angrily grumbled at him.

The polyglot moved forward, blocking Trepo and Zado from moving away from the gyrosphere from which Skopo proceeded to advance by himself.

Trepo gave his employer a cold, hard stare. "This is none of your business," he warned the owner of the Carnavan. "It has become necessary to take this person into custody for the safety and security of everyone, for we are all endangered by the potential violence he may commit here at the language school or elsewhere.

"He has been identified as one of the vandals destroying so many systems of viroid ribbons in Kalender. We must call the authorities and hand him over to the law as soon as possible."

Dari addressed an appeal directly to Frango. "Do not believe or trust this man who works for you as a waiter. He belongs to an underground group of conspirators who call themselves the Readers. They destroy and erase existing voidal systems of memory and communication in the name of a horrible, imaginary thirst for vengeance in the name of a forgotten viral inventor who claimed to have discovered the application of viroids.

"This language school is a recruiting ground for new members of the organization. You are fortunate that these criminals have not attempted to indoctrinate and exploit you for their nefarious ends."

Skopo now addressed Frango. "These Readers are satisfied to claim to be carnivores and use your restaurant as a place to assemble and plot together. But they have kept you ignorant of their true ideas and their criminal activities.

"I myself am a police detective investigating their organized vandalism. If you will allow me to call police headquarters, I can obtain immediate verification of all that I have been telling you."

"Is there a specific official who can verify what you claim?" asked the owner of the Carnavan.

Skopo gave him the name of Chief of Detectives Yato Pmom.

Frango studied the face of Zato Atat, then that of Trepo.

What conclusion was he going to reach? wondered all the others around him.

"We have to summon the police to straighten out these puzzling knots," he declared, his eyes taking the measure of Trepo and Zato with growing skepticism.

Skopo, moving fast, knocked the micropulser out of the hands of the waiter holding it. Mlem was able to scoop it off the floor, then hand it to the detective who had been imprisoned in a gyrosphere.

"I advise you to make an immediate call to the police for help," Skopo told the polyglot named Frango. The detective pointed the weapon that had been handed to him directly at the two flustered, confused members of the Reader conspiracy. "Do not try to escape or evade me and the micropulser that I now

hold. We shall now go with you to the director's office. I intend to question the two of you there."

"I will go with you and assist in watching and investigating what they have been up to," said the owner of the carnivorous restaurant

"I must contact my chief at once," muttered Skopo to himself and the others standing around him.

XVI.

Chief Yato Pmom arrived at the Atat Language School within minutes of being reached and informed of the situation and circumstances there.

A squad of plainclothes officers accompanied the official and took command of the school building.

Skopo described and analyzed the contours of the conspiracy he had uncovered and been the prisoner of.

"Dr. Predo Atat, the hydrophysician, is at the center of the Reader network and should be found and taken into custody immediately," recommended the detective who had been placed inside a gyrosphere. "His hope was to turn me into an ally who would carry out the plans and orders of the Reader commanders, of whom he was the leading one.

"He gave me over to his brother, the director of this language school. They intended to convert me into one of their agents, since I would be able to serve them from inside the police department itself. I would become a very valuable asset for them to make practical use of."

Chief Pmom gave several officers an order to take Trepo and Zado to central headquarters and grill them for names and identities of members of the general conspiracy that they had created and led in action.

"I hope that we can put a stop to the viroid erasures as soon as possible," he told Skopo and the Totmaxes.

"At last I know what the truth is," sighed Frango. "But I regret my blindness to what was going on. My waiter was at the center of their evil crimes, and I was totally ignorant of what was going on.

"But now I know and must stand against these people who call themselves Readers."

"The Central Library can now reopen without fear of further attacks," hopefully foresaw Dari, looking directly at Skopo. "We can never repay you for the risks you took with these mad men," she murmured to him.

"We have taken the snake and hold it by the head," the investigator told her. "Now, our task is to see to it that we leave none of the criminals escape our net to continue erasing viroid ribbons.

"My task will be to prevent this scourge from ever returning to Kalender or planet Farmer. That will take me a period of time I cannot estimate today."

"My brother and I know that you will succeed in that endeavor," softly said Dari, beaming a radiant smile at the detective.

Part III.

14 MAR

I.

Dari invited Skopo to dinner with her and Mlem that evening.

After an afternoon nap, he walked to their apartment. His strength and stamina felt completely restored. Street screens showed vidoid reels that told of police success in snashing the Reader conspiracy in Kalender. Communications and memory had recovered with incredible swiftness. The city was returned to normal.

Once the detective was seated at the Totmax table, Dari related a bit of news to him.

"The Central Library opens to the public tomorrow," she smiled with joy. "Mlem and I will be returning to our post and duties."

Her brother then spoke. "It was terrible, Skopo, how they tried to scramble your mind and make you one of them in the gyrosphere. There could have been permanent, profound damage to you, if it had gone on much longer."

"The police medicos did a quick scan on me at headquarters," revealed the investigator. "According to them, I show no signs of viroid toxicity. My body chemistry has returned to a normal stage."

"You were heroic in the sphere," sighed the librarian.

Skopo grinned. "All that I did was break out of the plastex bonds they tied me up in. Once my hands were free, it was plain what I had to do. I tampered with every dial, tab, filament, and gizmo inside the imprisoning globe."

"You never revealed your true identity or purpose to them," proudly said Dari.

"Dr. Predo Atat grew so outraged that he asked his brother to break my will by force. He had to know who I was and what I was up to. The more stubbornly I resisted, the more obsessed the hydrophysician became to crack me open. So, they brought me to the language school in an emergency cab, then put me into a sphere with a viroid ribbon that was meant to alter my mind completely."

"Meant to make you compliant and controllable, as weak as a sponge," muttered Mlem. "It was your fighting resistance that drew attention to your globe."

Skopo suddenly changed the subject. "What are we eating here tonight? I hope to return to standard vegetarian fare, now that I won't have to go to the Carnavan to eat any more."

"Ground bean salad, for a start," beamed Dari with a twinkle in her eye. "Then, some rice-filled bluepeppers. How does that strike you, Skopo?"

"I can hardly wait," he lightheartedly replied.

* * *

About the time that dinner was finishing, the apartment hummer sounded.

Mlem rose to see who was at the door. In seconds, he returned with Chief of Detectives Yato Pmom. The latter nodded in greeting to Dari, then spoke directly to Skopo.

"I have terrible news to give you: the Readers sent a battery of attorneys to headquarters with a court writ freeing the language school director, Zado Atat. His release has allowed him to disappear from sight, as his brother the physician has. We have no knowledge of the whereabouts of either one of them."

For a time, a sad silence filled the room as this was absorbed by those who heard it.

"And something else has come up," continued Yato. "Vnem Lenad has taken a turn for the worse. I have our agents watching and listening in the Hydroclinic. The man remembers you, Skopo, and says that he wishes to tell you something directly and personally. It may be important."

Kitanin sprang out of his chair. "I'll go there with you at once, sir." He turned to the Totmaxes and told them to proceed out ahead of himself.

❋ ❋ ❋

Two police agents accompanied the visitors to the flotation cell where the viroid engineer lay motionless, nearly expired.

A nurse in orange pants and coat hovered over the blue-faced patient.

Vrem looked up with an expression of futility. Not much time left to tell anything to anyone, seemed to be his mood and expression.

Slowly, words came out of the dying one's parched, swollen lips.

"…wands…meteoric…cave…"

Three words emerged, then a fatal blank.

Breathing stopped, eyes glazed, and stillness set in.

Vnem was no more alive. He would never again tell anyone anything.

Leaving him to the nurses to dispose of, Skopo and Yato departed.

"I have an idea where the Atat brothers may have fled," announced the Chief of Detectives. "They may be somewhere in the Meteoric Mountains hiding in a deep cave."

Dari stared at her brother, sending him a silent message with her face and eyes. She gave a small, almost invisible wink.

❋ ❋ ❋

Like a caterpillar attached to a string, the cars of the funicular train sped up the mountain side. The highest range of elevation on Farmer was that of the Meteoric Mountains. Of these, the tallest was Mount Meteor itself, a tower rising three miles into the purple sky. Only by special speed-train were the upper reaches in the heights reached. Tourists and vacationists came from all parts of the big planet for rest, relaxation, and inspiration in the yellowish snows of this unique mountain.

The train rose at an ever steeper angle, each individual car adjusting to the changes through appropriate compensating movement of the gyroscopic valves from which it hung suspended. The effect was maintenance of horizontal stability for the separate units making up the train. Like a crawling caterpillar, the series of cars climbed the vertical face of rock. The passengers inside suffered no pain or discomfort, but remained in nearly perfect equilibrium.

From a horizontal train, to a slightly inclined one, to a sharply-angled chain, to verticality. Each change was imperceptible to those riding inside.

Would this caterpillar become a butterfly when it attained the top? wondered Dari Totmax as she gazed out of the cablecar window, first downward and then up at the bright yellow snow.

Her brother, across from her, kept looking down into the valley they had ascended from. The long, fertile plain that stretched as far as Kalender served as the garden and breadbasket of the giant city. He and his sister were descendants of lowlanders, tillers of the flat farming soil down below.

All their lives, they had looked at the distant yellow snow of Meteor on the horizon. Now, for the very first time, they were to be in the highland itself.

Mlem sensed a breathless exhilaration inside his lungs.

The train began to slowly level out of its sharp ascent up the mountain side.

✻ ✻ ✻

Increasingly, the rocks and stones became horizontal. Skyslate cottages appeared, indicating mountain dwellers. Small hamlets flew past, surrounded by bluepine forests. The train straightened out, leveling itself.

All at once, the trees disappeared. Mustard yellow snow covered the barren ground. The heater in the train car began to clang, adjusting to the frigid coldness outside. Dari shivered a moment before the sharp chill vanished.

Train speed slowed. Passengers rose and stood in the aisles. Brother and sister eyed each other. Their destination had to be near, but the Totmaxes stayed seated.

"The snow is so beautiful!" marveled Dari. "No colorprint can do it justice. Notice how clean a blanket it makes."

The cabletrain came to a slow halt at a small, skyslate station.

Doors slid open and the passengers began climbing out into the perpetual winter of Mount Meteor. The librarian and her brother were among the last to leave.

Their baggage, by prearrangement, was on its way to the lodging house where reservations had been made for them. Mlem asked a conductor for directions to the Poets' Lodge. Once he had a sense of direction in the village, the pair started off past the foot-high yellow banks along the recently shoveled street.

Weather experts attributed the peculiar color of snow here to winds, altitude, and extremely low atmospheric pressure. Dari felt a strange excitement inside herself. Was it their high elevation or the mission that lay ahead for them? She was on Mount Meteor under false pretenses, as an amateur poet on vacation. Her aim was to improve her writing craft, she would claim.

Stopping in his tracks, Mlem pointed at a large chalet with steep roofs.

"That's the lodge," he calmly stated. "Let's go in and introduce ourselves."

The brother opened the silicon door for Dari, then followed her into a dimly-lit lobby that appeared empty. The two new arrivals surveyed the place a moment. There was nothing expensive or elegant here. Everything was old and used.

     VIROIDS

All of a sudden, a young woman of uncommon beauty appeared at the reception counter at the far end of the lobby. Bright yellow hair that resembled the snow outside framed a tanned, browned face. Mlem stared at her with awe. A devotee of the mountain sun, he had to conclude. A golden goddess of Mount Meteor. Her eyes were blazing sapphire, coldly indifferent to all going on in outside reality.

Dari told the receptionist who thus appeared who they were and asked her if their rooms were ready for them.

"Indeed," smiled the mountain beauty. "We have been expecting you, Miss Totmax. May I welcome you and your brother to the Poets' Lodge. Our hope is that your stay is happy and productive. I myself can hardly wait to have a look at your verse."

The librarian gulped hard. "Unfortunately, I didn't think to bring any of my writings along with me," apologized Dari. "My present aim is to write in a completely new vein, if possible. That is my purpose in traveling all the way to Mount Meteor. To start all over again. I mean to forget all my past scribblings."

The sapphire eyes grew absent and distant.

"That is the reason that I, too, came to the Lodge," whispered the woman behind the counter. For a moment, she was awkwardly silent.

"My name is Uraf Salint. I help manage the Lodge, as well as write. Perhaps I can be your guide up here on the mountain." She looked at Mlem, her eyes sparkling with purple light. "Are you, too, a writer?" she inquired.

"Not yet, but I am trying," he blushed. "I am only a beginner."

"Don't worry about that," chuckled Uraf. "Mount Meteor inspires creativity in everyone who visits here."

"I deeply hope so," uneasily remarked Mlem.

"Let me get your keys. I can show you your rooms," said the jewel-eyed poetess, moving from behind the reception counter.

Brother and sister exchanged glances while they awaited Uraf.

II.

Their rooms were small, spare, and comfortable.

Uraf took the two on a short tour of the lodge, showing them the laundry, kitchen, dining room, and memory library.

In the last chamber, she pointed out the dozen writing consoles on large silicon tables, turning on one of the display screens for them to see.

"If you wish, both of you can compose your work right here." She sat down at a keyboard. "Would you like to see me receive a verse of my own from the library's memory?"

"Yes," said Mlem with sharp interest.

"If it isn't any trouble," followed his sister.

"No trouble at all." Uraf typed in her personal code and brought up what she wanted to show. Immediately, a short stanza appeared on the viroid screen.

Dari and Mlem bent forward to read what it said.

"I came out of a dream,

Where everyone was dancing,

Where my dearest friend was death,

And time had no sides showing."

For a little while, neither reader dared to speak, or even look away.

Mlem went over the poem several times, as did his sister. Both of them seemed in a spell. What does this verse mean?

At last, Uraf herself broke the trance of the guests.

"Don't ask me what it means," she advised. "Please don't."

Dari gave a bewildered smile. "Why not, my dear?"

"Because I have no idea what to tell you."

Uraf pushed a side tab that erased what was on the viroid screen.

"You two are from Kalinder, I understand," she noted. "That is a city I have never seen. They say it is enormous in size."

"Yes, it is," confirmed Dari. "My brother and I work in a large library there. So far, our writing has been a leisure time activity. Do you come from the Meteor region, Uraf?"

The latter looked surprised. "No. It was only five years ago I arrived here from Plazh in the tropical zone. I grew up there, coming here to write."

"You were a visitor, then?" said the librarian with curiosity.

"I decided never to return home. Instead, I begged for a job and won one here. This is now the only place for me. My life and my work are tied to Mount Meteor. I doubt that I will ever leave."

"You have your friends here, then," purred Dari warmly.

Uraf's eyes gave off an unnatural purple glow.

"My viroid publisher will be here at the lodge for dinner together with all of our writers. That will give me a good opportunity to introduce you to him."

Both Totmaxes had the same question in mind at once. How does this publisher operate with poets?

As if psychic, Uraf answered that exact unspoken query.

"He has a system of instant publication over viroid cable. As soon as a poem is finished, Perek receives it in his memory bank. This makes it available to any reader on Mount Meteor who may wish to have a look at it. Anyone can read all of my work, even the most recent. And, in return, I have total access to everything that Perek publishes on viroid screens at all his other posts."

Mlem had a question. "Who is this person you call Perek?"

Urak turned her beacon eyes upon him. "Perek Tenrop inherited a fortune of incredible size from his family in the lowlands. But his preference is to work and live up here in the yellow snow of Meteor."

"He sounds interesting," remarked Dari with a grin.

❖ ❖ ❖

Deciding to explore the lodge on his own, Mlem slipped into the hallway and headed toward the memory library. As he neared the door of that room, he picked up a strange, sobbing sound. Was it crying? Stopping and looking in, he saw Uraf sitting at a viroid screen that appeared to be foggily blank.

The poet looked up at him as her new acquaintance approached.

"Is something wrong?" he asked her.

Her eyes had been dulled by copious tears.

"Two of my early verses are gone from the published memory ribbon. Completely wiped away. And those were my only recorded copies that exist." She gaped for breath, then sighed. "How can I recreate what was written years ago? So much has passed through my mind since then. I've written thousands of lines of poetry. How can a writer draw an exact version out of pure thought? Impossible to do."

Mlem focused on her sapphire eyes. "Can I do anything to help you?"

She suddenly smiled at him. "Thank you. But there is nothing that anyone can do for me at the moment."

The two studied each other a short time.

"I'll see you at dinner, Ulaf," he told her, quickly departing from the memory library.

He had news to report to his sister. Viroid erasure was present here in the yellow snow zone of Mount Meteor.

III.

Perek Tenrop scanned the dining room, then approached the table in one corner where Uraf sat with a group of writers that included the Totmaxes.

Tall, dark, and unusually tanned, the publisher carried himself with grace and assurance. His eyes were a gray that resembled mountain slate. Uraf introduced him to the new pair at the lodge. Tenrop shook hands with first Dari, then Mlem.

"Why don't we get in line so we can start eating?" proposed Uraf. "Most of you are probably as hungry as me."

The three at the table rose, following the lanky publisher into the cafeteria next to the dining room. The two females found places at the end of the fast-moving line. Mlem and Perek brought up the rear. Once they had their trays filled, the group returned to the table and began eating.

Uraf was first to finish. She looked across at her viroid publisher with painful emotion on her golden face. "I lost some of my poems today," she informed him, proceeding to provide details about the memory erasure.

Perek sent her a look of sympathy. "In the last week, there have been half a dozen cases like yours. I assure you, everything possible is being done to get to the bottom of these crimes."

Dari decided to pose a question. "Have the police been notified?" she said to the publisher.

Tenrop nodded yes. "But there are few officers up here in the yellow zone."

"There has never been such trouble on Mount Meteor before," added Uraf.

The publisher turned to Dari. "You must let me read some of your verses, Miss Totmax," he said with a smile. "I hope that I can be of assistance while you are here at the lodge."

"Neither of them has a publisher yet, Perek," revealed Uraf with a sly grin. "Perhaps you can do something about changing that situation."

Dari laughed. "I imagine you handle the works of an army of writers. Is your profession a very difficult one?"

Tenrop chuckled. "I enjoy dealing with my poets, but not the critics who depress and discourage them with their acidic attacks."

"Speaking of critics," interceded Uraf, "the worst one just entered the room."

For a moment, silence reigned around the table. The face of Perek Tenrop became bleak and expressionless. Dari noted how thoughtfully preoccupied the dark brown eyes of the publisher appeared for a time.

A short, fat figure who had just entered the dining room ambled slowly past their table, turning his large head toward the four as he neared them.

"Good evening, Uraf," the man called out in a high, tinny voice. "How are you?"

Everyone except the viroid publisher turned and stared at him. The poet took a second before responding. "I'm fine, Dioto," she coldly answered, not asking him how he was.

Both Totmaxes sensed the frigid hostility in her tone. This was a side of herself that Uraf had not revealed to the newcomers yet.

The round little man stared at the back of Perek's dark hairy head for a moment, then renewed his crossing of the dining room again, disappearing into the cafeteria.

Mlem looked at Uraf, while Dari stared across at Perek.

"That was Dioto Gerak," moaned the publisher at last. "He is a notorious scoundrel who claims to be a noteworthy literary critic. His reviews appear on several viroid tube channels, catering to the most intellectual part of the population. In my opinion, every line he has ever written on viroid ribbon has been worthless garbage. The imposter deserves to be driven out of this creative colony."

Dari and Mlem exchanged looks of unease. What were they getting themselves into?

Uraf began to speak to them in a hushed, secretive voice.

"Dioto is contesting Perek's re-election to the post of president of the Writers' Union of Mount Meteor. He is attempting to polarize the organization between the poets and the novelists. His only support, so far, has been among the short-story writers. In any way possible, the rascal has tried to sow bad feelings between the poets and the narrative writers. He has used his criticism to divide us into two opposing camps."

Dari thought of an idea that could put her and Mlem in good standing with the pair at their table. "If only my brother and I were voting members! We would certainly know whom to support for president of your Writers' Union."

Uraf beamed a smile while Perek seemed to flush red in the face.

"We would appreciate two extra votes for our side," said the poet. "If enough new writers joined us in time, we could defeat Dioto and his supporters."

The publisher frowned at Dari. "As soon as you have written something new, bring it to my office on the village square," he proposed. "I'll publish it on viroid ribbon at once."

"It may not have sufficient quality," objected Dari, all at once feeling beyond her depth.

"Let me be the judge of that." Perek then turned to Mlem. "And when you have something to show me, like several chapters of a novel, I would be more than happy to look it over."

"Perek desperately wants to get the two of you into the Writers' Union," muttered Uraf with a slight giggle. "He is eager for your support and votes."

The publisher glanced at the large timer hanging from the ceiling.

"It's almost eight," he announced abruptly. "The evening viroid dramas will soon be starting on screens. If we have all finished, we can join the crowd in the assembly room for big-screen watching."

"That sounds delightful," said Dari, looking at her brother.

The four rose from the table and Uraf led the way out of the dining room, into the main corridor, across the lobby, to the opposite end of the first floor.

The viroid screen was a gigantic one, covering a quarter of the outside wall of the room. Almost as soon as the group was seated, the images began to appear.

Multicolored figures suddenly drew the attention of the thirty present in the assembly room. All eyes centered on the enlarged face of a faraway announcer.

"Stay tuned to the Arts Channel for the premier of a new viroid drama never before seen on ribbons. It is a romantic comedy set two hundred years ago, with authentic period costumes and a musical score.

"But first, a report of late breaking news.

"Kalender police report a renewal of erasures of viroid memory banks in companies and agencies. These have been attributed to the group that calls itself the Readers…"

Neither Totmax dared look at the other. Both sat beside each other, pondering with inner excitement and fear. The vandalism they were familiar with in Kalender had not disappeared, but was arising there once more.

Dari and Mlem were unable to pay close attention to the historical romance on the screen as it progressed onward toward its end.

IV.

Dari, having promised the publisher a poem, rose after a few hours of sleep, took papex and pen from her luggage, and composed a short verse to present to Perek the following morning.

"I searched for a cave," ran the first line that she wrote down. She read over and over what she had. It was an idea that had captured hold of her mind's imagination. Where could the Atat brothers be, but hidden away under the ground?

The viroid vandals and their Reader followers remained as a constant obsession for her.

A poem about a cave might provoke or inspire someone to speak to her about the caves on Mount Meteor, Dari hoped.

Before dawn, she had completed the poem about what might be concealed in the caves of this mighty mountain.

* * *

A triumphant glow lit up the face of the poet as she and her brother finished their breakfast in the cafeteria the next morning.

Mlem was unable to conceal his inner qualms of concern as Dari recited from memory what she had created.

"I hope that it does the trick," he whispered to her under his breath.

Seconds later, Unaf walked into the room and made her way to where the Totmaxes were sitting.

"Good morning, friends," she smiled. "How was your first night with us?"

Dari answered. "Mine was wonderful, because I managed to finish off my first poem written on Mount Meteor."

"Congratulations!" exclaimed Uraf. "Perek will be happy to see the result. We can go to his office as soon as we are finished here. That will be better than reading the poem to him by viroidline. He will want to talk with you about the publication and the terms of payment."

"Payment?" said Dari with surprise. "I have to pay, then?"

Ural stifled the laugh rising up her throat. "Not at all. It's the other way around."

"I receive the payment?" asked the still puzzled librarian.

"Remember, Perek possesses a fabulous amount of wealth. His family left him a fortune impossible for him to exhaust. It grows as fast as the fellow spends his viroid credits. Yes, he pays each of his poets according to the quantity and quality of their writings. Usually, the two are in inverse ratio. The more verse someone produces, the less value each line has. Some of the best creators here on Mount Meteor have turned out only a limited number of ribbon pages, yet their work is prized and acclaimed beyond that of the ordinary rank of writers of poetry. One can never tell which way a newcomer will go, small quantity but sublime quality, or the other way around."

"I see," said Dari with a sigh. "It will be interesting to see what Mr. Tenrop thinks of my work," she added.

Uraf excused herself in order to go through the short cafeteria line.

The brother and the sister exchanged silent but meaningful looks.

❂ ❂ ❂

Mlem agreed to stay at the Poets' Lodge while Uraf took Dari to the office of the viroid publisher. It was best he nosed around there, finding out what he could in conversation with the other residents.

The two women put on snowboots and went out into the slushy yellow-tinted street. A weak wind was blowing down from the slatestone cliff above. Neither poet spoke as they passed forward. No one else was out or about in the cold.

Uraf steered her walking companion toward the entrance of a brickstone building of a dull coppery brown hue. She opened and held the door as Dari stepped into a warm lobby, then went in behind her.

A secretary working at a small desk rose and started toward a door further inside.

"Mr. Tenrop told me to show you right in," she chirped in a high soprano.

As the three females reached the metallic door, it opened from within.

Perek, in a magenta leisure suit, stood tall at the opening.

"So glad to see you two," he called out to them. "Please come right in. I hope you have something ready to be published, Miss Totmax."

The secretary returned to her desk as Perek closed the office door behind his visitors. He pointed to two plastex easychairs. As the poets sat down, the publisher went back to his own chair, behind a long, low dark desk made of silicon.

"Where shall we start?" he sang out soothingly.

This fellow seems in a very good mood, Dari told herself in private.

Uraf explained that her companion had a verse to present to him.

Perek eyed Dari with intense curiosity. "So soon? Would you like to recite it aloud for me?"

"That's the way it will have to be given," murmured the librarian. "I do not even have it committed to paper in final form yet."

"Proceed, then," he directed. "I am listening."

For a moment, Dari was unsure how to go on. She decided to use a formal but subdued style of vocalization.

"I searched for a cave,

Beneath the banks of yellow snow,

Where I might bury my merciless memory.

But each time I seemed to find one,

The cave was full of the markings,

That other minds had abandoned there."

Dari waited for reaction from one of her listeners. Surprisingly, the first comment came from Uraf.

"I like the way you maintain your momentum," she smiled, looking directly at the author of the verse. "It moves along well, keeping the form concise."

"Thank you," replied Dari, her eyes focused on the viroid publisher. He remained mum, his brown eyes vague and abstracted.

At last, he moved his lips. "Let's get it down at once. I want to send this poem out to our subscribers today."

Dari had a choking sensation about her vocal organ. "Thank you," she managed to say.

"First of all, a contract will be necessary," declared the publisher as he rose from his chair. "I will get a copy of the standard agreement for you to sign." He went to the door and exited from the office.

The two visitors exchanged broad grins. "I'm so happy," gushed Dari. "I didn't know whether the poem would be any good."

"It was outstanding," whispered the other. "Never lose your originality, but nurture and preserve it."

When Perek returned with the papex contract, Uraf rose from her seat.

"I must return at once to my post at the lodge. You should have no problem getting back there, Dari. Just remember the route we took coming here."

The publisher suddenly made a proposal. "I'll follow my newest writer back there later. That will allow me to have lunch with both of you."

"Fine," noted Uraf, moving to the door and departing.

Perek handed the contract to the librarian to look over before signing.

"It appears satisfactory," she said as she quickly scanned the document.

❀ ❀ ❀

When their legal business was ended, Perek Tenrop all of a sudden became introspective, leaning back in his chair and staring at his new client poet.

"People often wonder why I came to Mount Meteor and set up this publishing enterprise. It's quite simple. I truly enjoy helping in developing and encouraging original talent. It became clear to me long ago that I was never going to be a creative artist of any kind. My disappointment depressed me, until this substitute activity presented itself. Although I myself would never write anything of value, it was possible to become a sort of midwife for the outstanding talents and gifts of others. Fortunately, the material means left me by my family were more than adequate for this life mission of mine."

"So, you made yourself the patron of a series of creative writers," grinned the newest poet. "That, I believe, is something to be highly proud of."

The face of Perek seemed to pale and stiffen. "But I am not on the same level as individuals like you and Uraf. Your work has the greater intrinsic worth." His brown eyes looked beyond her, to the panorama window revealing the yellow snows of Mount Meteor.

The viroid publisher changed the subject abruptly to a matter important for Dari and her brother.

"Your poem focuses upon caves and what may be hidden in them," he told her in a low, subdued tone of voice. "Were you thinking of the famous ones on Mount Meteor? They present a big attraction for the visitors at our tourist centers in the yellow snow zone. You must have been quite aware of them when you were composing this poem of yours."

"I've often read about them," she explained. "They have become a sort of symbolic image in the interior of my mind."

"There are motor-sleds that take passengers out on tours that include many of the caves. Perhaps you would enjoy entering some of them with a group."

"It sounds interesting," she said with enthusiasm.

Perek stared past her, at the snowy scene outdoors. "You should be starting for the lodge," he suddenly recommended. "A heavy snowfall appears to be beginning."

Dari turned about and gazed out through the panoramic window.

* * *

Flakes of incredible size of a brilliant, chrome-like hue fell and swirled through the frigid air, making any walking difficult. The mountain was a place of visual fantasy as the librarian trudged toward the Poets' Lodge.

If it were not for the cold, she might have stopped to enjoy the eerily fascinating yellow scenery. Billions of pieces of frozen water floated down with reluctant slowness, inducing an almost crazed distraction in her thought.

Downward wafted an endless amount of precipitation, covering the street cobbles leading to the lodge now buried in yellow. Dari thought of curtains, infinite veils of an unnatural fabric, hiding some secret of an evil nature.

She remembered how Uraf's sapphire eyes had looked when describing the destruction of her archive of poetry. A crime against creativity by the wands of the Readers, that is what has broken out on Mount Meteor. A bitter taste came up into the mouth of Dari.

Sooner than expected, she reached the entrance door to the Poets' Lodge.

As she extended her right arm to open it, someone pushed it open from inside.

It turned out to be her brother, who had seen her approaching through the snow from his bedroom window. He had hurried there to help her come in. His face was red with excitement, she noticed at once. Had something happened while she was gone?

"A disaster..." he stuttered once she was inside the hallway. "Complete erasure of all the published poems of all the writers staying here at the lodge."

Dari, still covered with yellow snow, opened her mouth with astonishment. In seconds, she realized what had to be done at once.

"We have to find the critic, Dioto Gerak," she asserted with all her power of will. "He is the one everyone here will be holding responsible for this."

V.

Mlem found a directory of viroidfon numbers at the reception counter. The address they were after was listed under the name of the literary critic.

"It's at the opposite end of the village from the lodge," he sighed with vexation. "The storm is still in progress outside. Should we make a call to him?"

"No," advised his sister. "The best course is to visit him there as soon as conditions clear up outdoors."

Writers saddened by their tragic loss of past works had congregated in the dining room. A few were weeping. Others were making arrangements to leave the lodge and the mountain as soon as they could.

Putting on his snowcoat, Mlem stepped out into the now clearing air. The yellow snow had ceased descending. The wind was quiescent. He returned inside and related the conditions to his sister. The two decided to make the trek that they thought was urgent.

The Totmaxes tramped with energy through the narrow street, past the village square, to the farthest section of the writers' colony. By the time they reached the small cabin where Dioto Gerak made his home, the last sign of the storm was gone. The mountain appeared placid and still once again.

The pair hastened to the front door of the bluepine structure. Mlem, finding no hummer or ringer, knocked on the wooden door with his fist. No response came for a considerable length of time, until a voice from inside sounded sharply.

"I'm coming! I'm coming! Be patient a little while, till I get there."

Mlem instantly quit rapping on the hard pinewood surface of the door.

The wait for the door to open proved a short one. Dari sensed the growing impatience of her brother. All at once, a red-haired head extended outward out of the cabin.

Dioto Gerak glared in anger at Mlem. Then, catching sight of the sister, his fierceness softened and subsided. Self-control suddenly prevailed in him.

"Don't stay out there," his metallic voice commanded. "Step inside my house."

Dari led the way in. The critic closed the door behind the pair.

Gerak studied her face minutely, as if confirming a judgment made originally at the moment he had first seen her outside at the entrance.

"I know who you are," the fat little man confessed. "You've read my review of your verse, then?"

For a moment, the poet was confused, until she realized what he was referring to.

"No, I had no idea that you have already evaluated the poem that Mr. Tenrop said he was going to publish on viroid ribbon. It was this morning that I presented it to him, a very short time ago."

Dioto made a nasty sneer. "It took me only one simple reading to see how derivative your little piece of work is. I broadcast my judgment on the Writers' Union viroid net within a few seconds of my judgment."

"I haven't had the opportunity to see your criticism, sir. That is not the reason my brother and I came here. Are you aware of what has happened to the memory banks at the Writers' Lodge?"

Dioto's baby blue eyes squinted. "No, tell me."

Mlem answered him. "Every line these writers have ever published is now erased. There are no papex or celluloid copies. Thousands of poems are gone forever."

The critic made a sour, mocking face. "It's no great loss to the literary treasury of Farmer, my boy. Most of their work is weak and meaningless. My opinion of what gets published by merchants like

Tenrop is negative. He has the money with which to make himself popular with the untalented hacks he publishes on viroid ribbon."

"This happened even earlier with Uraf Selint and her poetry," protested Dari. "All her verses are now destroyed and gone. She was the first victim, perhaps a test run. But now all the lodge residents have suffered total erasure."

Dioto gave her a haughty look of scorn. "This Uraf is a wholly bad writer. Her poems were without merit of any sort. I fail to see any reason to regret what happened to them."

A fist of the brother rose into the air and in a second or so would have smashed into the pie-shaped face of the literary critic. In time, Dari lifted a hand and grabbed the wrist of outraged Mlem. She succeeded in avoiding collision and harm.

"We must leave at once," she mumbled in a crackling voice. The two visitors exchanged looks as the cabin-owner took a step backwards.

Seeing sense in what she said, Mlem turned about and followed her to the door. Without a word to Dioto, the two exited out into the yellow-covered street.

As they headed back to the Writers' Lodge, Dioto Gerak watched them from behind the plastex curtain of the front window of his bluepine cabin.

✦ ✦ ✦

The wind still howled from time to time, but without the earlier blizzard force. Not until they approached the chalet where they were staying did the sister dare to speak.

"We must not let anything divert us from our objective, Mlem," she reminded him. "Our mission is to locate and destroy the source of all the viroid erasures."

Mlem's silence signified his acquiescence in this opinion of hers.

They took off their boots and snowcoats in the lobby. As they made for their rooms, a familiar face appeared at the end of the long corridor.

Perek Tenrop raised his right hand in greeting and to attract their attention.

"Where have the two of you been?" he asked as he stepped closer. "Uraf is resting in her room, but she suffered a close call out in the snowstorm. The wind brought her down in a deep drift."

The two Totmaxes rushed briskly to where the publisher stood outside the door of the lodge manager, Uraf.

Dari provided him a concise explanation of their absence and the visit they had made to confront Dioto Gerak at his cabin. "We saw no sign of Uraf anywhere. What has occurred with her?"

Perek pursed his lips. "Listen while I tell you what happened. Several residents reported to me that she planned to go and express what she felt to Dioto. But it appears that the poor soul didn't reach there. That could have been due to the fury of the snowstorm.

"Uraf fell into a culvert and was found there when the blizzard ended. A passing pedestrian caught sight of her bright orange coat and went to the rescue. Her hands and feet nearly suffered frostbite.

"A police snow sled was sent to bring Uraf back here to the lodge. I was summoned and hurried here at once."

"How is she?" anxiously asked Mlem.

"Resting in a coma," solemnly announced Perek. "The village medic just left. He thinks that sleep is the best thing for her now. The sedation given to Uraf should only last till dinner time this evening."

"Any injuries suffered?" inquired Dari.

"Nothing that can't be quickly repaired. But tell me this: how did Dioto Gerak receive you when he learned who you were?"

"He was insulting and supercilious," frowned the new poet. "He has already reviewed my poem and stamped me as an untalented, imitative clod."

"That is outrageous," muttered Perek.

"The erasure of Unaf's life work meant nothing to that beast," she shivered. "Her poetry seems to have no value at all to him."

     VIROIDS

"Damn him!" cursed the publisher, his face flushed with red. "Damn the bore!"

Mlem had an idea of how to calm down the emotional fires. "Why don't we go to the cafeteria and have some bush tea," he suggested. "We can discuss these matters there."

❀ ❀ ❀

There were only a few writers eating when the trio entered. The latter group obtained cups of mountain herbal liquid, then sat down at a corner table.

"Whoever is behind the memory destruction may have a very simple purpose in mind," darkly began the publisher.

"What could that be?" asked Dari from across the table.

"Bankrupting me and putting an end to my publishing business."

Mlem leaned forward. "You are losing a lot of money, then?"

Perek nodded yes. "Subscriptions to our ribbons are already down, and much more loss can be expected. People no longer wish to read what I publish."

"Your operations may fold, then?"

"My firm, the Poet's Lodge, and this entire creative colony may eventually be gone."

"If Dioto Gerak is behind what is going on, what could his ultimate goal be?" said Mlem as if to himself. "Is he some sort of madman bent on decimating and ruining the writers gathered here on Mount Meteor? His motives may be too twisted for any normal mind to comprehend."

The viroid publisher took a sip of bush tea before sharing what he thought.

"All I know is that wild ambition reigns within this critic. He craves to become the great man of literature on our planet. The presidency of the Writers' Union is only one steppingstone on his upward trajectory. There is no limit to the heights he dreams of, believe me. Ambition has made him wild and unscrupulous. I doubt that Mr. Dioto Gerak has any trace of a conscience within him."

"The election of president will take place soon, won't it?" quietly murmured Mlem.

"The day after tomorrow, in the evening," said Perek. "The voting will take place by secret ballot here in the lodge, in the dining hall."

"Do you think that you could win the election?" whispered Dari, staring at him.

The publisher hesitated. "I don't know for certain," he admitted. "I just cannot say, one way or the other."

*　*　*

Only in Dari's room could the Totmaxes speak in secret.

"What next?" asked the brother in a lowered tone.

His sister thought a while, her eyes turned away from Mlem. When her decision was made, she revealed it to him.

"We must find out when a snow sled will leave for the main caves and reserve places on it for ourselves."

The pair gazed directly into each other's eyes, communicating in silence.

"Shouldn't we send a message to Skopo in Kalender?" soberly inquired Mlem. "He has heard nothing from us, so far."

"No, it is best that we wait till we have definite, concrete evidence to offer him."

The brother thought for a few moments. "Very well," he concluded. "I'll go around and find out what transportation is available for us."

VI.

Uraf opened her sleep-filled sapphire eyes, attempting to orient herself. She was in her room at the lodge, lying in her bed. Who were those people watching her so intently? She studied the faces and identified who each person was.

Dari, Mlem, and Perek were the individuals present near her. They were observing her awakening. She made a strenuous effort to remember what had recently occurred. Why did she have a feeling that something very terrible had happened to her? Uraf asked herself. Why were her thoughts and emotions in such turmoil?

Outdoors, she had gone into a terrible yellow snow blizzard. Slipping, she had fallen to the icy ground. Wind blasts had tortured her with sharp pains. A long, blank period of sleep had followed. When and how had her consciousness revived? she wondered.

"Don't say a thing," whispered the publisher of her poetry. "Just try to rest and gather strength. You are still weakened and injured from your horrible experience. Just stay still and continue to rest."

All at once, Uraf remembered the viroid tragedy that destroyed her life work. Her eyes darted about in different directions, finally settling upon Mlem.

"Bring me some pieces of papex and a handpen from the lodge office," she begged with humility. "I need to put something down right now."

The Totmaxes exchanged questioning looks. At the same time, Perek moved forward to the side of the bed. "What are you going to do?" he asked her.

"I remember now why I wanted to see and talk to you," groaned the poet in bed.

"You wish to write something down?"

Uraf nodded. "My memory of recently written poems is still alive in me. I want to get them down as soon as is possible. I should never have become dependent on viroid ribbons and storage memories, with no records in reserve. But the mind that composed the many poems that were lost can perhaps restore some of them."

Mlem moved toward the door of the bedroom. "I'll get you what you need," he said as he stepped away.

Dari moved nearer the bed. "We will help you recreate all that your mind can recover," she told the one in the bed.

After Mlem returned with the writing supplies, Perek excused himself and headed home. The Totmaxes found chairs and sat down as Uraf began to write something.

Within a minute, the latter had rewritten one of her favorite poetic creations.

She gave it to Mlem to read, a victorious smile on her pale face.

His eyes slowly perused the spare, loose six lines.

"Never repeat, always go forward,

Do not linger when you can leap

Over the boundaries, into what some

Might wish to label terra incognita,

But which I know to be

My one true native land."

Mlem, staring at the writer, handed the sheet of papex to his sister.

"It is phenomenal!" he gasped with unconcealed excitement.

Uraf gave him a smile, then returned to the work that now engrossed her mind.

❋ ❋ ❋

By next morning, there were over thirty verses down on papex.

Dari and Mlem had gone to their rooms after midnight, thoroughly exhausted. They agreed that Uraf was on the way to recovery, both physically and mentally. But their own special, secret assignment on Mount Meteor remained unfulfilled.

Rising early the next morning, Dari went to the Poets' Lodge office and used the viroidfon to call Mountain Tours at a nearby tourist village. Yes, there was a motor-sled going through the region that morning. Yes, it could stop at the Poets' Lodge to pick up two extra passengers. This was the slow season, and there was plenty of room on the vehicle. Be there waiting at the entrance to the chalet at eight o'clock. Yes, the tour included a number of the major caves on Mount Meteor.

Dari checked on Uraf, who was placidly asleep and would in all probability remain so for the rest of the day. This was their opportunity to move about the caverns till evening. What might they discover in them?

The motor-sled was a ten-seater, low and streamlined, with a transparent silicon canopy that permitted total viewing of the yellow snow landscape.

Behind the lethargic driver at the controls, there were only two others aboard beside the Totmaxes. There would be plenty of chances to wander about on their own. No one was going to herd them about like gawking children, both Dari and Mlem agreed. They would enjoy a great degree of independence.

The two strong, sharp polymetallic skates of the sled glided over the fields of yellowish snow as if they were on polished ice. Upward toward the peak of the mountain climbed the sleek winter carrier. The sky was a brilliant light gray color. All indications were that the day was to be free of storms.

Mlem looked rightward, his sister to the left as they sped over the snowscape. Each of them was trying to foresee what might lie along this journey they were on. Both were surprised when the driver abruptly cut the speed and announced that the main cave area was immediately ahead. They had arrived at this important destination earlier than they expected.

The two other passengers, young newly-weds on their honeymoon, were first to climb out of the motor-sled. As the Totmaxes passed by the driver who was standing by the open hatch, Dari spoke to him in a gentle voice.

"I was told that it would be quite alright if we explored about on our own," she cooed. "Any objections to that?"

The driver shook his head. "No," he replied with a sweet smile.

As soon as they were standing on the packed snow, the Totmaxes surveyed their surroundings. A high ridge above, a deep gorge below. The path to the nearest cave had a white polymetal fence guarding it on both sides.

Dari noticed something down at the bottom of the mountain gorge and pointed at it. Mlem looked below, then at his sister.

"What is it?" he whispered to her.

She spun around and walked back to the motor-sled. The driver inside opened the hatch for her.

"We can see a little building down in the valley. Does someone live there?"

"That old shed?" laughed the man sitting at the controls. "Only an old recluse hides out there. I've only seen him a couple of times, at a distance. The spot is protected from winds, but it is a terrible way to live, if you ask me."

"Thank you," said Dari with a grin. "We were just curious."

She made her way back to Mlem and the two proceeded along the fenced trail. Since the newly-weds had already entered the nearest cave, they went on to the second one. Its mouth was narrower and not as high as that of the first. A small plastex sign hung to the side, a few feet from the entrance. It read "Light Tubes".

Mlem stepped forward and pulled several of the tabs on a leverboard. Whitish illumination filled the interior of an enormous cavern beyond the entrance. The roof spiraled upward like a temple dome. Mottled walls extended into the distant end of the cave.

"Let's go in and look about," said Dari in a hollow voice.

* * *

The caves were gigantic, but empty of what they were hunting for.

Each of them contained light tubes, but no sign of human activity there.

Cave followed cave, each like the previous one. Their search appeared futile to the pair after the seventh cavern was inspected.

"Either there is nothing here, Mlem, or else we are making some terrible mistake."

"What are you thinking, then?" said her brother.

Dari pondered a moment. "Perhaps Vnem Lepad meant something different from what we understood him to be telling us. What if he intended to say that the location was under the caves rather than what we took his directions to be?"

Mlem became both confused and excited. "Under the caves, beneath the caves, or in the caves? What was he trying to say with his last breath?"

The sister stopped and peered down into the gorge.

"Let's have a look at this hermit's shed before going on into more caves," she told him.

* * *

They zigzagged on, past rocks and snow banks, their view of the destination growing clearer and more defined. There was much more here than a simple shed. A mountain cabin of chiseled slate walls and a bluepine roof. This was a larger structure than it had appeared to be from a distance. Why had the driver called it merely a shed?

The building seemed still and empty. But there were marks in the yellow snow that indicated some kind of movement or traffic. A sled? wondered both explorers.

As they drew ever closer, signs of occupation became visible.

Boot prints on the packed yellow snow around the place. Narrow skate tracks.

No, there was more than a lonely recluse who used this location.

In complete silence, the snoopers approached the door facing the nearest of the caves. Should they knock or try to open it and enter at once on their own?

What if there was someone inside who might present a danger to them?

Without hesitation, the pair proceeded to the threshold of the cabin. Each step forward was slower than the one before. Since they had come this far, there was nothing left but to risk everything. Mlem glanced at Dari, who gave him a single nod of the head. Go on, she signaled him. Open the door so that we can have a look inside.

Faster than it could be thought through, the deed was done.

A front room with confortable plastex furniture, warm, neat, and up-to-date. Walls covered with pink-colored papex. Not at all the expected den of a mountain hermit.

From somewhere inside, a voice they had recently heard now spoke to them.

"Come in, come in. If you are so curious as to travel here, you deserve to have a good look around."

From a corner chair, rose the familiar figure of the driver of the motor-sled. The burley older man moved toward them. "Please close the door behind you," he added.

Sheepishly, the intruders filed into the parlor of the structure. Only then did they see the viroid micropulser in the man's right hand.

"Tell me what you two are looking for. There is no cave in here."

The driver moved closer and closer.

Neither the brother or sister showed any sign of fear or alarm.

"I'd like to know what you thought was hidden in here," growled the holder of the tiny weapon.

The next sound was that of a door in the rear of the room opening.

A tall male in a green sleep suit emerged. His eyes were a sleepy yellow.

In an instant, Dari and Mlem identified him as someone they had met in Kalender.

It was Zado Atat.

VII.

Skopo Kitanin had both good and bad news to report to his chief.

As he entered the latter's office, he could sense that this was going to be a crucial, decisive meeting where the future course of his investigation would have to be settled.

Yato Pmom motioned to him to sit down. "What is the current status of the case?" he began.

"Here in Kalender, all but a small handful of Readers have been captured and are now held in custody. But reports of spreading viroid vandalism continue to come in from other directions, especially the coastal area. Something entirely new is starting in the city of Plazh. The viroid ribbons of cable entertainment and fliko-films are the most recent targets of the terrorists. This has never happened before. It is an escalation on the part of the Atat brothers, from printed material to drama presentations. So far, neither the fliko industry nor the Plazh police have been able to cope with the growth in criminal destruction by the Readers that remain."

"I see," mumbled the Chief of Detectives. "What about this trip that your friends from the Central Library took to Mount Meteor? Anything from that quarter?"

"No," frowned the investigator. "So far, not a word from them."

Yato, deep in thought, said nothing for a considerable length of time.

"Things are now under better control in Kalender," he finally decided. "It is possible, I believe, to send you to Plazh to help the police there with your experience handling the Readers."

Skopo's face brightened. Something like a smile crossed his mouth.

"One thing more, sir," he gently said. "Could I go to the coast by way of Mount Meteor? I would like to see for myself how the two

Totmaxes are doing there. From the beginning, I've had questions about sending amateurs up there."

"They volunteered. In fact, the pair threatened that they were going to travel on their own, privately, to look into the last words spoken by Lenad, the viroid engineer."

"I know," nodded the detective. "They pressured me into allowing them to go."

"Very well, then, take an extra day on the journey to Plazh and stop to see how they are doing up on the mountain."

"I'll leave within a couple of hours, sir," said Skopo, rising to his feet and hurrying swiftly out of his superior's office.

❋ ❋ ❋

The vertical caterpillar ride held little interest in itself for one of the passengers aboard. Skopo's mind was on what he intended to say and do once he reached the Poets' Lodge.

From the funicular station he followed directions to the chalet where his associates were staying. His heartbeat quickened as he approached, then entered the Poets' Lodge. Seeing the reception desk, the detective marched boldly up to it. From here, he could see through an open door into the office where a woman sat at a table with a viroid screen upon it. Her head turned and a pair of unusual eyes focused on him.

The sapphire color of her pupils was the foremost and most noticeable thing about the female rising up and walking toward him. Then, the pale gold of her face. She moved to the edge of the reception desk and looked directly at him.

"Yes, can I help you?"

"I am looking for two friends of mine who are staying here at your lodge. Their name is Totmax. They are brother and sister, called Mlem and Dari. I know that they will be eager to see me."

Her hands clasped the edge of the desk as Uraf braced herself.

"I am sorry to have to tell you that they have been missing persons since yesterday. Please come into my office so I can describe what is known about their disappearance."

❋ ❋ ❋

An excursion to the mountain caves. Wandering off on their own, without informing the driver-guide where they intended to go. Not showing up for the journey back, even though the motor-sled waited an extra hour for them to appear.

Once it was concluded by evening that the pair were lost in the yellow zone, the Alpine Corps was summoned to mount a hunt for them. Because of darkness, the search was delayed until daybreak. Rescue sleds began patrols in the cave region. All available snow vehicles not in use were mobilized and covered numerous ridges and valleys on Mount Meteor.

Uraf went on to describe Dari's success as a poet who had been published over viroid ribbon.

Skopo gave her his name, but not his profession or official employment in Kalender.

His mind whirled like a spindle. He had to take action, he realized. Perhaps more aid had to be called in from outside. The situation here was threatening and dangerous for his two partners, he said to himself with dread.

Could the cover of the Totmaxes have been somehow destroyed and their purpose here exposed to view?

Had they found something of interest in the zone of caves?

The investigator rose to his feet. "I would like to talk to the person in charge of the Alpine Corps in this district, Miss Selint," he announced in a firm tone of voice.

"That is Captain Bukk. He has many years of rescue experience in the yellow zone. His diligence in search expeditions is legendary, and he is sending out all the motor-sleds possible. The local police are cooperating with their glidecopters as well."

"When may I see this officer?" pressed the detective.

"The president of our Writers' Union, Perek Tenrop, is in constant viroidfon contact with him. We will be having an election meeting this evening in the lodge assembly room. All the writers of this community should be present because our presidency is at stake.

"So that Perek can keep fully abreast of the situation, Captain Bukk called here a little while ago to say he was coming to our cafeteria for lunch today." She glanced at the wall-timer above Skopo for a moment. "That will be in about half an hour."

"I'd like to talk with both your president and the captain," requested Skopo. "Perhaps I can be of some assistance, since I know both of the missing ones."

* * *

Caves for tourists and vacationers to visit, with deep under them especially constructed mining tunnels that were unused, abandoned, and nearly forgotten existed in the yellow snow zone.

Early settlers on Farmer had included prospectors for ores of value on other planets. Much was too little or too difficult to extract. Fortunes had been made by a few speculators sinking tunnels on Mount Meteor. But most mining ventures had lost everything and proved unprofitable.

Concealed mines and tunnels were available for secret purposes. This had drawn the Atats and their Readers to the cave region. Not the open caves, but what was hidden beneath them.

Viroid light tubes illuminated the rock walls of certain special tunnels. Lifters rose and descended chosen shafts used for criminal purposes. A small city of vandals occupied an area under the mountain caves.

The two Totaxes found themselves locked by their captors in a tunnel where Reader supplies were stored.

There was plenty of time for Mlem and Dari to put together what they had so far seen and heard.

Zado Atat was in league with the motor-sled owner who had driven them here. How many other snow-vehicle operators were providing criminal transport for the organized vandals?

They had glimpsed what appeared to be a workshop. Artisan hands were busy with the construction of viroid-equipped wands. This was a stronghold of the criminal nihilists, where they operated what resembled a factory.

The brother and sister communicated in cautious whispers, sharing ideas and emotions. They were able to perceive the colossal enmity of their enemies, their profound drive to destroy the world of the viroid.

Revenge without logic or limits was the threat coming from these tunnels. Retaliation had run amuck. Destruction had become an end in itself, not a means to vengeance or some form of justice.

"We are dealing with obsessed people!" opined Dari, shaken completely.

"Their very insanity may be what makes them so devilishly clever," muttered Mlem. "The outlandish nature of their ideas gives them a strange, powerful vision. The Atat brothers are not stupid or ignorant, not at all."

Hopeless desperation seized hold of both of them.

VIII.

Captain Bukk proved to be small and slight.

His only source of authority was the power of his stentorian voice. He wore a simple snowsuit under his heavy siliconweave coat.

Uraf introduced the friend of the Totmaxes to the district director of the Alpine Corps as he came to their table in the cafeteria. Behind him was a tall, thin man with dark brown eyes. The publisher of Dari's first verse, president of all the writers of the lodge.

Skopo shook hands with the Captain, then Perek Tenrop.

All four took seats around the small, square table.

"So, you happen to know Dari and Mlem very well," began the publisher. "They did not mention family, relatives, or anyone else."

"I have been close to them for years," lied the investigator. "They told me by viroidfon to stop and see them on my way to the sea coast. I have business waiting for me in Plazh."

Uraf addressed a question to Bukk. "I take it no sign of them has been found. Is that correct?"

"Sadly, you are right," said the alpinist. "I will be returning to the cave region immediately after leaving here."

The detective saw his opportunity and reached for it.

"Could I go the area with you, sir?" he requested. "The frustration of inactivity drives me to distraction. I would lose my mind if I had to sit still and wait for news to filter in on its own."

The sincerity of such a statement seemed to impress Bukk, a good judge of character.

"If you wish, there is an extra seat in my motor-sled."

"Perek and I have to stay here at the lodge and prepare things for tonight's meeting and election," said Uraf with regret on her face and in her voice.

"You shall be kept informed of any developments," promised the Captain.

He then turned to Skopo. "If you are ready, we can leave at once."

The two took leave of the poet and the publisher. They walked out of the cafeteria, down the corridor and across the lobby, and out of the chalet.

"I have never seen a disappearance so complete and traceless," remarked Bukk as they seated themselves in the Alpine Corps motor-sled. "It's as if these two individuals had been snatched off the surface of Farmer."

Frowning with apprehension, the detective made no comment at all.

* * *

The prisoners had just finished eating the meal brought them by their Reader guard and then given back to him their food trays. They were both surprised by the unexpected appearance of Zado Atat in the tunnel in which they were held.

"What do you think of our facility", cynically inquired their captor. "This is a perfect base from which to carry out our operations. Although visitors come to the caves above us every day, no one ever suspects that the Readers have a workshop and storage warehouse down below in these forgotten, abandoned mines. We enjoy cover from any prying officials or policemen."

Dari decided to take a daring tack. "What villainy are you planning for us?" she demanded. "What awaits us in your calculations?"

Zado grinned slyly. "My brother and I are fully aware of your maneuvers, such as the pretense that you are creative poets. You came to Mount Meteor as imposters, but our organization quickly unmasked what your true purposes have been from the start. We have our people where we learn such things."

He glared at both of the Totmaxes in turn with bitter hatred on his face. Then he spun around and moved toward the lifter that had brought him down to this particular tunnel.

Dari and Mlem looked at each other questioningly.

"What now?" asked the brother.

"I would guess that Predo Atat is not at present in the immediate vicinity, so that Zado does not wish to decide our fate on his own. But that situation may not last much longer."

"Is there anything we can do before then?" pleaded Mlem. "Some way of signaling to the outside? I'm sure that there are people searching for us. The Poets' Lodge has certainly informed the yellow zone police of our absence."

The two of them were silent, listening to a faint, distant humming sound. Each was aware that the other heard it, since it had been audible, on and off, for hours.

"A ventilating device of some kind," muttered Mlem.

His sister furrowed her brow. "Where there is an air pump, there must be a vertical pipe or shaft for inflow and outflow."

"I doubt we can scale it from this far below."

"Perhaps," mused Dari. "But what if enough smoke could be generated to fill it up? Enough to send a distress signal out into visible air above ground?"

Mlem raised his eyes and scanned the tubs, barrels, crates, and boxes that filled most of the tunnel they were imprisoned in.

"Yes, I believe we could start quite a fire with what is available about us," he declared, rubbing his chin with his right palm.

❋ ❋ ❋

From high on a yellow ridge, Scopo and Captain Bukk peered down at the strange building in the gorge below them.

"Someone is living in that?" said the detective from Kalender, pointing out the old, decrepit cabin.

"I myself inquired and found a reclusive loner inside. The man wouldn't allow me to enter, only speaking at the door. He reported that he saw nothing and no one because he sleeps most of the day. An unfriendly, uncooperative character he was. We have quite a few such antisocial individuals on the mountain. They move here to be free of external control. Anyone knocking at their doors will be considered to be disturbing their peace and solitude."

You have lived on Mount Meteor all your life, then?" asked the investigator.

"Indeed. I joined the Alpine Corps when I was only sixteen and had already seen hundreds of rescues from the snow. But nothing like this situation near the caves. The brother and the sister must have wandered off in this direction. But I can't understand or figure out why they did."

Skopo considered his options a moment. "These caverns have been thoroughly searched by your alpine patrols?"

"Yes, in the first hour of effort on our part."

"Do you have any objection if I take a walk about on my own, Chief?"

"Not at all," murmured Bukk. "You might pick up something that others have missed."

* * *

The first three caves that were entered by the detective proved disappointments.

It was the fourth one that had something noteworthy about it. At first, Skopo was unable to put his finger on what produced a strange sensation within a part of his mind.

There was a faint smell of acidity. An odor of something burning. He sniffed again and again. That's what it is, he told himself.

Skopo moved swiftly toward the dark area in the rear of the cavern.

The single light tube overhead ended in solid shadows ahead of him.

He took a tiny penluxer out of his pocket, pushed the cell tab, then proceeded with its brilliant rays guiding him.

Deeper and deeper he penetrated, avoiding sharp rocks and stalactites.

The smoke that he had previously smelled was now visible. He raised, then lowered his penluxer, searching for its point of origin. Black plumes were rising a little way before him, as if out of the floor of the stone-faced cavern.

Several times the terrible stink made Skopo cough and retch. Still, he continued advancing toward the source. His steps slowed as he reached what appeared to be an opening with a fine metallic wire grating over it. His throat choked as he knelled on his knees to examine what he had discovered.

There was a shaft below the floor of the cave. Where did it come from? What was burning with such speed inside the interior of the mountain?

It was obvious to him that this was a human artifice, the result of someone's conscious plan. What was its function and where did it originate?

A voice buried within his mind instructed Skopo to call loudly into the smoke-filled opening.

The words he yelled into the black shaft came out of his throat with primal emotion.

"Dari, Dari. Where are you? Is this smoke a signal from you?"

From far below, the sound of a male voice reached his ears. This was followed by one within the female range. The words were not understandable for a brief time. Only gradually did he make out what the voices were trying to communicate.

 VIROIDS

Help. Danger. We are in an old mine tunnel. Readers. Zado. Danger.

Inside the mind and thoughts of the knelling inspector from Kalender, the connecting synapses sparked to life with nearly explosive electrical energy.

As each word came to be deciphered, his intelligence came to life.

Skopo cried out one word to the pair who had caused the smoke and fire: "Coming".

❋ ❋ ❋

Surprised and stunned, Captain Bukk saw the needs of the situation in a flash. He gave the detective a searching look.

"Why didn't you tell me that you are a policeman from Kalender?"

"In order to maintain the cover I took when I decided to travel here. It was necessary to conceal my purpose on Mount Meteor so as not to frighten off the Readers."

Bukk nodded that he perceived the need for the silence. "I can muster patrol teams at once," he said, pursing his lips.

"The only way into the tunnel that is known to us is inside the cabin," went on Skopo. "Do you believe it can be quickly captured by your people?"

The Captain bit his lip. "I can foresee a frontal attack at full speed at the cabin, simultaneously from all directions. Coordination of our movements will be a vital necessity."

"The safety of the pair being held must be given top priority," argued Skopo with nervous force. "That is so, even if it means escape for some of the Readers."

"We shall attempt both the rescue of the captives and the capture of the criminals," promised the alpine commander. "My hope is to possess a general measure of success through the advantage of surprise. We must take the risks involved in what lies ahead."

"There exists a net of mine shafts and tunnels beneath many of the caves, then?" inquired the detective.

"That is what our land charts indicate," frowned Bukk. "Until now, none of us in the Alpine Corps took these conditions seriously." He glanced at the timer on his right wrist. "In a few minutes, the snow teams will be in position for the assault on the Readers."

Part IV.

18 MAR

I.

Dari looked away from the fire that her brother was feeding papexboard into.

The Reader approaching the two with a tray of food saw at once what the prisoners were up to. Smoke from the controlled blaze could be smelled by him at once, impelling the little man to drop the tray and reach into his pocket for his tiny micropulser.

"Stand where you are and don't move," commanded the guard in gray pants and jacket.

The Totmaxes looked at him in terrified surprise, then turned their eyes on each other. What were they to do under these circumstances? Were they going to suffer irremediable harm?

All of a sudden, Mlem took action, picking up a plastex rod and crying out to his sister "Behind the fire! Quickly, on the other side!"

Instantly, Dari dove in back of the red, orange, and yellow flames. At the same time, her brother rushed forward toward the open doorway, surprising and almost for several seconds paralyzing the Reader who was holding a weapon.

"Stop!" screamed the man in gray. "Don't come any closer."

Mlem heard these words, but it was too late to do anything else but proceed with his desperate attack. Onward he threw himself, threatening to collide with the Reader and knock him over. Even though he heard the shouted warning, he pressed on. It was impossible to cease and halt.

Dari watched from behind the dancing flames as her brother leaped upward toward the shaking hand that held the little pulser.

A rippling sound, lasting less than a second, occurred just before a loud thud.

The Reader stepped forward and kicked the plastex rod out of the hands of the inert body sprawled on the floor of the tunnel supply room.

Dari, her heart palpitating wildly, saw the guard approach his now receding foe.

"Come out from back there," barked the armed one. He waved his pulser about as if at random. "Don't do anything foolish, or you'll get the same as he did."

❋ ❋ ❋

Dark purplish clouds filled the late afternoon sky over the lonely cabin in the slatestone gorge. Captain Bukk had assembled and stationed his forces. The police officer from Kalender insisted on being in the command sled with him.

"I have a small arm that I can shoot, if necessary," explained Skopo. "But the alpinists, of course, will make up the first line of assault. That is understood by me."

His seat was in the extreme rear of Bukk's vehicle. He was to be primarily a witness, but not necessarily an active participant in what was soon to happen.

The Captain carefully checked his personal timer, then spoke to the driver of the motor-sled.

"Only a few more seconds to go. All eight of the snow-sleds are in position and ready to move," said Bukk. "One of the scouts up on top of the ridge will fire flares in the air for a while. That will signal the start of our charge toward the objective." He paused and drew his breath. "Speed will be most decisive in this. The time has arrived for action."

Concentrated silence reigned within the command sled. Scopo had direct view of the entire valley that was about to be crossed by the invasion force.

The faces of the crewmen in yellow coats were focused upward toward the rim of the ridge above the caves. Patient, concentrated waiting abruptly ended. White flares rose into the air.

Captain Bukk ordered his driver to gun the sled's motor. From eight different positions, the dash for the hermit's shack started. The attack was meant to be strong and relentless. Surprise would be an important advantage to the police.

Skopo had never realized that a snow vehicle was capable of such lightning-fast motion. He watched as the dilapidated building came closer and closer.

The decisive confrontation had now arrived.

II.

Dari glared with scorn at the grandson of the self-styled inventor of viroid ribbons as he was given a sketch of what had transpired below in the tunnel.

The Reader guard had hurried her into the lifter, up to the above-ground cabin. Mlem lay below, wounded and bleeding where he had fought.

"You have caused me a great deal of inconvenience and trouble," grumbled Zado Atat. "The time has come to put an end to your interference."

At that moment, the walls of the building suffered a great quaking shock.

Zado and the three Readers in this command center looked about in stunned wonder. What was happening? they silently thought as they gazed at each other.

Outdoors, the attacking sleds had the cabin in a tight noose.

Alpinists were tumbling out of hatches, setting up a perimeter line around their target.

Groups of arms experts placed plastex-powder charges onto the bluepine walls of the structure, then stepped away.

One by one, holes were blasted on each side of the cabin.

Through clouds of debris, dust, and powder, men and women armed with pulse weapons entered the interior of the ruin. Only one of the Readers had the presence of mind to raise a pulse-shooter in opposition. He was instantly hit and felled by a particle shot.

"Up with your hands!" commanded the first alpinist to reach the cabin office.

Behind the first and second lines, Skopo caught sight of Dari rushing forward toward her rescuers. She held her right arm high in the air.

But another figure, Zado Atat, was also running toward the blasted front door opening.

In a split second, Zado seized her around the waist, attempting to make the woman into his shield against the rescuers.

Dari screamed with all her vocal power, then struck Atat with a clenched fist before he succeeded in pushing down her arm and grabbing hold of it.

Captain Bukk, running up fast, raised his pulser and fired it once.

Fortunately, he was an experienced, expert marksman. He knew how to hit a moving target with accuracy.

By the time Zado was sprawled on the floor, Dari had made it through the doorway and out into the open.

In seconds, the detective from Kalender had the librarian nestled in his arms. He assured her that she was now safe.

All at once, she thought of her brother down below. "Mlem…he was shot down in the tunnel where we were held. Let me show you where the lifter is."

Skopo and the Captain followed her into the corner where she pointed out the mechanism that would take them to where her brother lay wounded and injured.

* * *

Seriously injured, but still breathing, Mlem lay on the tunnel floor.

Dari and Skopo watched in silence as the wounded brother received emergency treatment supervised by Captain Bukk.

A crew member came forward and whispered to the Captain. The latter turned to the detective. "The leader of the vandals just died. We will have no more trouble from him."

In five minutes, it was possible to move the patient up to ground level. Bukk made the decision to transport Mlem to the district hospital by motor-sled.

Dari asked to go with him. "I can't leave him alone at this moment," she insisted.

"I wish to make an immediate search of this place for documents and evidence about what the Readers were up to," decided Skopo. "Their organization may still exist in other localities and areas. Dangers could persist elsewhere."

Once the speeding sled had departed with the Totmaxes, Skopo and Bukk started a search of the communications center of the cabin. There were records of messages from Plazh and messages to Plazh. Going through the drawers of a desk, the investigator from Kalender began to reach conclusions.

"I believe that the center of Reader attention and activity is now in the city of Plazh," he told the Captain.

Examining the contents of a filing case, Skopo discovered evidence of the targeting of libraries, banks, stores, and factories on the sea coast.

All of a sudden, he came upon commands issued to a person on Mount Meteor.

The name of the recipient was in coded form, but Skopo quickly deciphered its meaning. Again and again, the word "Pornet" appeared in orders and documents.

Pornet will accomplish this in time. Pornet has completed instructions sent to him. Pornet carried out a successful raid on poetry memory. On collected writings of a certain poet.

All at once, the investigator realized what fascinated his thinking about what he was reading in the Reader file.

If the name "Pornet" was reversed from front to back, it spelled "Tenrop".

Skopo was stunned by the implication of that fact.

❀ ❀ ❀

In the conference room of the Poets' Lodge, a large crowd of writers had assembled for the election of a new president. Every member had received a secret ballot on which to record a choice. Dioto Gerak sat in one rear corner. His opponent, the publisher who already held the top office, was in the front row among his supporters.

Uraf Selint had agreed to preside over the meeting while the ballots were collected and counted.

The members impatiently twisted and shuffled. Suspense mounted, for this was known to be a very close contest this time. Nervous energy filled the air.

All of a sudden, all eyes turned to the back of the large hall where something unexpected was occurring.

A number of alpine officers, led by Captain Bukk, had entered and were watching what was going on in front.

Skopo Kitanin entered, boldly marching up the central aisle to the rostrum where Ural stood, waiting for the results of the vote tally.

The detective nodded to her, motioning that he wished to tell her something.

All eyes in the room centered upon the two of them.

Perplexed and confused, the presiding poet stepped forward to where the intruder stood.

Whispers occurred between Skopo and Uraf. The latter flushed with astonishment. She suddenly pointed to the first row, specifically to Perek Tenrop. The latter sat there surrounded by his supporters.

The president of the writers' Union leaped to his feet.

Seeing this, Bukk and his team rushed forward along the two side aisles and up the middle one. Perek, spinning around, caught sight of the group closing in on him. He lurched toward the door in back of the rostrum where Ulaf stood.

In an instant, Skopo ran up beside the cornered publisher. His right hand grabbed hold of Tenrop by the forearm. His left bent around the man's neck.

VIROIDS

He kept hold of the viroid vandal till the alpinists reached there and arrested the publisher.

The Writers' Union had never before witnessed such a scene as this.

*　*　*

A motor-sled came up to the Lodge in the darkness. Skopo, waiting in the lobby, rose from his chair and rushed to the door to open it for Dari.

She looked the detective directly in the eye.

"Mlem is recovering," she announced. "His prognosis is very good."

"I'm so happy to hear that, Dari. Come over and sit down. A lot has happened that you will want to hear about."

Once they were both seated, he swiftly described the arrest of Perek Tenrop.

"The members decided to make Uraf the new president by acclamation," smiled Skopo. "The other candidate, Dioto Gerak, had withdrawn his name."

"I am so happy for her," remarked Dari. "But what will happen to Perek now?"

"I foresee many years of imprisonment in the sea islands for him."

"But he seemed so trustworthy!" she burst out. "It was Dioto Gerak who appeared evil and suspicious to Mlem and me. The publisher seemed to be poetry's best friend. There appeared to be nothing shadowy or suspicious about the man."

Skopo sighed. "My work has taught me to ignore initial impressions and external appearance. What we see or think we see is only an assumed mask. It could be that Perek had an envious mind that the Readers managed to exploit. The Atats knew how to bring twisted personalities into their web of influence. Consciously or unconsciously, he aided poets. But deep within his mind, he was a destructive devil, mad with jealousy of others with creative attributes and characters."

"Zado Atat can do no more harm to anyone," solemnly said the librarian.

"That's right, Dari. But his brother remains at large and still operates. I plan to leave tomorrow morning for Plazh. There is a rising wave of viroid raids there, centered on the fliko industry."

"Be careful, Skopo," she warned. "The Readers remain still dangerous."

"Yes, I realize that."

"I wrote a short poem about our adventure on Mount Meteor," she told him with a pensive smile.

"I'd like to hear it, Dari."

She recited it from memory for him.

"The evil I feared to see,

Is now detected and uncovered,

By one who dives and delves deeply,

Into mountain caves and tunnels,

And finds smoke signals,

From the invisible sources."

III.

Skopo surveyed the giant studios of Plazh from the porch of his hotel room. They were famous for drawing the young and ambitious to the city on the Azure Sea. He reminded himself why he had traveled here by train. What lay behind the vandal attacks upon the viroid entertainment industry? I have to talk with the most important producer of dramatic ribbons in this city, the investigator said to himself.

* * *

The main office of Gax Productions was a donut-shaped high rise of ivory white silicon. Skopo made an appointment to see the head of the fliko conglomerate, Tandem Gax.

The latter was a long, stocky giant with a square head that resembled a slatestone rock. His hair was straight, short, smooth, and black.

"Sit down, Mr. Kitanin," his bass voice rang out. "There is a lot I would like to tell you."

The viroid mogul sat back in his gigantic, throne-like metallic chair.

"I have been receiving anonymous warnings over viroidfon for some time. They tell me to stop all ribbon production, or there will be destructive consequences. Because I ignored such threats, vandals have struck with erasures. Their targets have been the prompters used by our performers. Are you familiar with how these operate?"

"The prompters are viroid projectors that feed actors their lines. A script appears in legible form, beamed into the eyes of the performer."

Gax frowned. "Already, entire viroid plays have been wiped out. Studio production is increasingly impossible. The losses are unimaginable."

"This has all the earmarks of the Readers," asserted the detective. "Their motive is vengeance upon our modern viroid technology. The claim is that all of our developments have been illegal and unjust, the results of fraudulent theft. These fanatics convince themselves that they are victims of a conspiracy that stole the field of viroid application from its original creator."

"Other fliko companies have received similar threats and destructive damage. Our entire industry is in peril. But the police are unable to uncover the culprits. The vandals are as clever as they are evil."

"I would like to look about one of your studios, sir," proposed Skopo. "My experience fighting these vandals can provide me hints of what to look for."

The producer grew excited. "My daughter is in the cast of a drama currently being recorded. She plays the main female romantic role."

"It would aid me a lot to witness how a dramatic program is put on ribbon," said the visitor.

"I shall make the arrangements for you, then," promised the head of the studios.

❋ ❋ ❋

The romantic drama scene being recorded was in a thick tropical forest.

Tall plantain trees rose among papayas, boniatos, and kaboches.

Only one actor stood in front of the viroid camera. Skopo was beside it, listening to the soliloquy of the short, slim brunette with eyes of hypnotic green. Her voice was slow and dreamy. She spoke as if in a sleepy spell.

All at once, her green eyes appeared to turn dark, becoming almost black.

Her mouth widened and remained open. Nothing came out of it as she stared into the viroid recorder.

Skopo turned to the producer standing beside him. Gax was moving quickly toward the small group congregating around the camera.

Something had gone wrong. The tall, skinny director had risen from his chair and advanced into the jungle set. He spoke to the confused, lost actress.

"What is it, Teba? What made you stop that way?"

Out of her gaping mouth flowed a fearful stuttering. "My lines were gone. I didn't know what came next. It was chaotic for me. I fell into total confusion."

Tandem, walking onto the set, came up to the pair.

"Did the prompter go blank?" he anxiously asked his daughter. "Is that what stopped you?"

"That's it," she whined. "Nothing came forth on the viroid ribbon."

Her father took her hand in his.

"There will be no more recording today," he announced loudly. "I'll have you taken home at once." He turned to the lanky director. "Let's go to your office, Mizo. I want you to meet someone." His right hand pointed at Skopo.

❋ ❋ ❋

The detective tried to size up the director as they were introduced.

Seeing him out on the street, it would have been impossible to guess his profession. A director was supposed to be potent and commanding. Not this Mizo Harn. A boney scarecrow, there was nothing artistic or creative about him.

Something invisible told Skopo not to underestimate this viroid director.

"My operators believe the entire script was vandalized," groaned Harn. "My writers will have to make an entirely new ribbon, starting from scratch."

"We will lose at least a week," said Gax. He turned to Skopo. "You think you know who is doing this to us?"

"It has all the marks of a cult of vengeance-seekers called the Readers."

"I have read press reports about them," muttered Mizo. "I don't understand what their motives might be."

Skopo made a grimace. "Once such a form of madness is born, it evolves onward on its own and becomes ever more vicious and criminal. The Readers are far ahead of our conventional viral memory technology. That is why there is almost no defense against their attacks. We have to capture them in order to stop their destructive erasures. They will never put an end to the insanity that has taken hold of them."

The detective studied the face of Mizo as he turned to Gax and addressed him.

"I hope that Teba is well enough to attend the reception for my father tonight. His jetboat arrives this afternoon and I will be picking him up at the harbor later today. Why don't you bring Inspector Kitanin along with you?"

He turned his head and looked at Skopo.

Gax smiled. "Yes, I'm sure Taba will be well enough to be there." He turned to the detective. "Mizo's father is coming from the Peculiar Islands. He is head of the famous Mesmeric Drama School there. I expect to see a lot of the luminaries from the entertainment industry at the reception. Would you like to get to meet them?"

"Yes," smiled Skopo. "It sounds like an interesting evening. There is much about the drama recording industry I could learn that will be helpful in my investigation."

"I can take you in my cruiser," said the mogul. "Mizo has a nice villa on the coast, a short distance from Plazh."

IV.

On the luxury boat cruise along the coast, Tandem Gax told Skopo what he knew and thought about his star director.

"Mizo has always fascinated me. He came to our company as an assistant writer. I was on the lookout for raw talent and he gave me some of what he had put together out on the Peculiars. The material was very good, so I hired the promising young dramatist to work for me.

"His great grandfather ran a traveling comedy group. And his father was founder of the Mesmeric Drama School. Some of our best actors have been trained there under classical hypnotic control. That is a method that originated in the Peculiars and is still alive there. Long before the invention of the viroid prompter, direction of actors was occurring under trance control of the memory. But today that system has been replaced by viroid ribbons and projection techniques.

"When Mizo informed me that his father, Kanm Harn, was going to visit Plazh, I asked to meet that authority on acting methods. There may be a lot he can tell me from his years of experience."

The cruiser slowed and approached the dock of the luxury villa.

❖ ❖ ❖

Kanm Harn had the stage presence of a seasoned performer from the age before memory ribbons. He bowed before Teba and kissed the hand she extended to him.

"I have enjoyed your work," he beamed. "We try to keep up with the latest in viroid drama on Eerie Island where I live. You are a beloved star there."

As his son introduced him to Skopo Kitanin, Kanm gave him a fixed stare.

"You are with the police in Kalender?" he said with surprise.

"I am helping deal with certain crimes affecting the studios in Plazh," grinned Skopo.

The face of Kanm turned frigid. "Yes, my son told me about what is happening. It is tragic. But such crimes become possible when complex technology is applied to dramatic production. Things used to be easier and safer in our field. There was less complexity, and therefore less confusion. Problems tended to be much fewer."

Tandem spoke up. "You must visit our studios, Mr. Harn. I want you to see how we produce so much of what I call quality entertainment."

The white-haired Kanm gave a sorrowful look. "Only by limiting how many pieces are staged can the highest quality be maintained. Too many dramas in too short a time are a recipe for problems."

No one made any comment on what the veteran of the stage had just said to them.

Tandem Gax introduced Skopo to production executives, distributors, technicians, and writers from his company's studios.

Teba took over the guidance of the detective. "Come with me into the library," she said to him. "I have invited all of our acting crew in there for an informal get-together."

Skopo entered with her, noticing that Kanm Harn was the hub of a group forming about him. All of a sudden, the man from Eerie Island broke away and walked over to speak to Teba.

"I wish to tell you about a project I have outlined to my son, Mizo. It is my main reason for having come to Plazh. He pleads that he is too busy, being tied up at your studio. What I want him to do is bring his viroid unit to our island.

"There would be no need for artificial sets. We have a diverse, colorful natural setting all over. I want him to record all of our traditional dramas there. Costs will be much less expensive back there on any of the other Peculiar Islands.

"We do not use viroid prompters, so production will be free of these reported erasure attacks. My staff will quickly train the studio actors how to apply the hypnotic method in their stage work."

Teba gazed at him with a stunned, glassy look. "My father will be the one who decides on such a revolutionary matter. Has he heard of this plan of yours?"

"Not yet. That is why I tell you first, Miss. My hope is that you convince him that it makes sense in view of the present situation in Plazh."

Unexpectantly, Kanm turned to Skopo. "Perhaps you can help make Tandem Gax see the wisdom of moving drama production to the safety of the islands," he softly said.

With that, the main guest returned to the circle of actors who were his fans.

Teba and Skopo exchanged inquiring looks in silence.

V.

As the cruiser carried them back to Plazh, Teba told her father about how Kanm Harn had described his project for drama production in the islands.

"He wants to win the agreement of his son, Mizo, as well," she concluded. "He has not won that yet."

Tandem turned to Skopo. "What do you think, Mr. Kitanin? "Would we be free of sabotage if viroid prompters were replaced by hypnotism?"

The investigator grinned. "I know almost nothing about dramas and acting. It is a decision that those in your industry must make for themselves."

"More news of erasures came in during the reception," moaned the producer, turning to his daughter. "Would you be afraid of entering mesmeric trance, Teba?"

"Not at all," she smiled. "It would be a totally new experience that would take me into new areas of acting. I believe that it would be highly interesting and exciting.

"I want to talk this over with Mizo, then reach a decision," announced her father.

❋ ❋ ❋

Teba and Mizo each talked to Tandem Gax until he agreed to have their unit move from the Plazh studio to the Eerie Island. His only demand was that Skopo Kitanin accompany them for the sake of safety and security.

"There will still be viroid cameras with ribbon in them there," he insisted. "The mesmeric method of prompting is only a partial protection of the dramatic enterprise."

The sea trip by motor launch took most of one morning. From the harbor, it was only a short walk to where they would be staying, the old and ornate Colonial Hotel. Down the same street was the Mesmeric Drama School, as well as the personal cottage of Kanm Harn.

After settling into his room, Skopo went down to the gigantic lobby with lush tropical furniture and decoration. The Harns were going to take him and Teba to see the drama school, then to dinner at a famous local restaurant.

A viroid screen flashed news from Plazh near where he sat down.

Several important studios had to be closed because of erasures. Vandalism was causing enormous financial losses in the ribbon entertainment industry. The city was terrified for its future.

Skopo failed to see Mizo approaching him from behind.

"It looks bad on the mainland," groaned the director. "Let's hope we can escape this plague here on Eerie Island."

The detective spun around. "Teba should be down soon. I've been waiting for her. She told me she is anxious to begin acting once more."

Mizo grimaced. "The erasures in Plazh have greatly disturbed her. Perhaps her nerves will calm down here. I sincerely hope that she can pull herself together out here on this island. She is an actor with natural talents she was born with."

At that moment, the actress appeared at the bottom of the stairs from above.

* * *

Skopo ate a passion fruit salad, dryrice soup, and a jungleyam casserole with his companions. As the group finished its fruitgel desert, Kanm turned to Teba with a question.

"Have you ever intentionally, consciously been placed into a trance, my dear?"

She gave a slight start, but collected herself and tried to make a reply.

"No, I have no memory of anything like an hypnotic state. Never in my life."

She attempted to avoid the fixed, unmoving gaze of the old man.

All at once, from the other end of the table, Mizo spoke up in a ringing voice.

"The mesmeric methods have advanced quite a bit since I started out at the school," he asserted. "Remember, father, at that time even you relied on the traditional talking form of entrancing. Today, all of that has been transcended."

Kanm nodded yes, his eyes still on Teba. "That was a slow, simple method back in the past. There was no need for technical apparatus of any sort. It all depended on the skills of the mesmerizer as an individual."

"What was the old way like?" inquired Teba.

"Complete silence and semi-darkness," murmured Kanm. "You asked the subject to do some deep breathing for a while, to attain a quiet body. A shining globe could concentrate the mind. A ticking metronome was useful. Attention had to be totally captured and fixed. That was the first step.

"Muscle relaxation and the sensation of monotony had to be induced, with the final result being drowsiness. Calm security replaced all signs of stress.

"Then, I would talk as gently and sympathetically as possible. I asked the actor to unburden his or her mind to me. Forget your body, make all your senses quiescent. Let your eyelids do as they want. Do not tell them what to do. The goal was to limit the field of consciousness, producing a state of abstraction, of absentmindedness. Passive receptivity developed. I often made passes with my hands or stroked the forehead. Once the trance existed, I began to teach the lines of the drama part. At that point, it became quite easy to accomplish. The actor absorbed the drama like a sponge. It occurred efficiently, without any difficulties at all."

Kanm focused on Teba, with Skopo and Mizo following every word of his.

"I now have an effective instrument to facilitate this method. My name for it is the viroid mask. It can be placed on the face of a subject preparing to play a role. A deep trance captures control of the mind within a few minutes. Then the mask itself teaches the part to the actor. In less than an hour, all the lines and moves are completely mastered. This is far ahead of the older system that was used in the past."

Teba asked a question. "It's safe?"

Kanm chuckled. "Yes, my dear. We have lost no one using the mask. It contains primarily memory ribbons with viroid material."

"The viroid mask must be a new device, because I am certain it is unknown elsewhere," suddenly interjected Skopo.

"Yes," nodded the head of the school. "Mainlanders have never had much interest in mesmeric science. But it is part of our historic culture here in the Peculiar Islands."

"I am extremely interested," announced Teba, "and can foresee myself trying to make use of such an aid to actors in mastering their lines."

VI.

Skopo walked to the Drama School the next morning with Mizo and Teba.

"You shall be a pioneer," the director told his star actress. "No one else in the studios of Plazh has ever used this viroid mask of my father's. The first one shall be you."

In the school's practice chamber, Knom introduced the three of them to his mesmeric technician, Tuko Tara. This was a tall, bald, and dangerously obese islander who seemed drastically distant, abstracted, and preoccupied. He gave quick, perfunctory greetings to the visitors from the mainland.

"Shall we begin?" proposed Knom with a grin. "Let's show Miss Gax how the mask works."

The mask lay on the top of a silicon table. It had a brilliant white facial surface.

"As you see, it has the appearance of a traditional Eerie Island ritual mask. That makes it easier to recruit local actors into using it.

"Why don't you try it out, Teba? We can then go on to your first experiment in using it.

"You will learn, through the viroid mask, the role of Royal Princess Bota. The drama to be staged deals with the conflict of islanders with spiritworkers from the mainland. The local inhabitants considered them to be witches.

"The princess you play tries to learn the methods of the outsiders who come to live on Eerie. The results are tragic. Bota loses everything: her lover, her parents, the island throne. But she applies the secrets of the spiritworkers in order to drive them into the Azure Sea.

"It is a long, convoluted drama of thirty acts and eighty separate scenes. The public has always loved it, but it exhausts and overpowers the entire cast.

"The viroid mask solves all these problems. Each actor comes to have perfect mastery of her or his part. Confidence rises high on stage. All the lines are spoken smoothly, fluidly, without self-doubt or fear."

"Everything is ready, sir," announced Tuko. "The actress can take the seat and I will place the mask upon her."

The technician picked up the white mask and carefully fitted it onto Teba.

Skopo noticed the gossamer viral strings that connected the mask to a small terminal placed on the table beside the actress.

The body of Teba relaxed and she gradually fell into semi-coma. The line learning in a trance began, taking only several minutes to complete.

❈ ❈ ❈

Skopo did not enter the Colonial Hotel, but continued walking past it.

This was his opportunity to look about the harbor. He sensed that there might be things of interest to him there. This was more intuition than logical analysis.

Small pleasure boats and fishing skiffs were lined up on the pier. Workers were making repairs on several of them.

A sign over the door of an old building drew his attention. "Morphic Dormitory" was what it offered to the passersby.

A long, dark room with garishly violet lighting presented itself. It took the detective several seconds to adjust his eyes to the strange redness.

A sound that reminded him of sawing reached his ears. It had to be snoring men.

Out of nowhere, a voice came. "What do you want? All my bunks are taken by these daytimers. There's no more space in here. You came too late."

"I'm only looking around," muttered Skopo. "I don't want any space."

A hideously disfigured face approached through the reddish light.

"Then why did you come in?" growled a deep bass. "You look like a mainlander to me. What are you after?"

"I'm a visitor on Eerie Island. But I want to leave as soon as possible."

"Take a ship or a skyboat, pal. Don't look for your fare in here."

"You don't understand. No public means of transport will do. Only a hired rafter can get me where I want to go."

"Is that what you're after? A boat available for hire?"

"Exactly," replied Skopo with an enigmatic grin.

"Come back tonight. I know someone who might be willing to help you. Be here about eleven and be alone."

"Right," said the intruder, turning and hurrying out of the dormitory.

VII.

Teba was tired and went to bed early that evening. The two Harns were busy with scenery at the school. Skopo slipped away from the hotel and headed for the Morphic Dormitory. He had his appointment with an unknown transporter by small boat.

Can an investigator operate by means of hunches?

He wondered how it was that the Readers struck and disappeared with such speed. They seemed to be invisible and ghostlike. Their coming and going seemed wrapped in mystery.

What if they arrived from over the Azure Sea, on fast craft? Where might they have a hidden base during daytime? The Peculiar Islands, such as Eerie? wondered the detective from Kalender.

The underclass around the docks could possess some valuable secret information that would lead him further, Skopo told himself as he walked down the rockstone pathway to the docks. Only a few strollers were out, mostly men on the prowl. The smell of cheap herbal beer flowed out of dusty bars. Drinking songs played on local instruments floated through the evening air.

He reached his destination and opened the door. Snoring rose from the sleeping bunks. The same lurid red lighting fell from ceiling tubes. The smell of unwashed male bodies reached the nose of the visitor.

All of a sudden, a female shape jumped out from between two beds and stood in front of the newly arrived Skopo.

"You were here this afternoon and asked about hiring a boat?" screeched her high, rasping voice.

She was a short woman with a large, honey-colored wig. Her sensuous red dress had a provocative flavor. Who was she, and what was her business here? Skopo attempted to guess.

"I would like to have a serious talk about how to reach the mainland without using public transport of any kind," he calmly whispered. "Can you help me, or take me to someone who is able to do that?"

Large, almond eyes stared through the red glow. "Follow me," said the shapely female in blazing red. "The dulser is waiting in the back."

The Dulser? pondered Skopo as he walked behind the red dress. Who is the person she calls the Dulser? It took a small time to adjust to bright white light. His guide disappeared once the two men faced each other.

The little man studied Skopo with his bright hazel eyes.

Within less than a minute, he learned this person was a kelper who dealt in seafood and owned his own small vessel.

"There is nothing unusual for me to take passengers to the mainland. I have transported persons I know, but never a stranger. That would be something entirely new for me," muttered the short stranger in a seaman's clothing.

"Are there boaters who regularly take unknown travelers over the sea?" inquired the detective, eager to find out more on the subject.

"Indeed, there are," admitted the Dulcer. "I have a friend who does it all the time. In fact, he collects very little kelp. Transporting is his main business.

"I am busy with sea harvesting at this season, but I could talk with my friend about what you are seeking. What do you say to that?"

"It would be good for me to meet with your friend," proposed the investigator with a warm, sweet smile.

"He can meet you right here tomorrow morning," grinned the Dulcer. "His name is the Hiziker."

Skopo shook the hand that the stranger offered, then turned about and left.

VIII.

The transporter was waiting in the back room of the Morphic Dormitory.

Small and light of weight, he was not at all what the detective expected.

"You are the one looking for a rafter to take you across?" The Hiziker looked Kitanin over from head to shoes.

"Let's take a little stroll down by the docks," suggested the boatman.

The pair left the flop-house and headed for the old wharf on the other side of the harbor. Neither said a word till they reached a quiet, deserted spot and sat down on an isolated bench.

"You are a mainlander, I take it," began the Hiziker. "Why are you so interested in hiring a boat to Plazh?"

Scopo improvised an answer. "Let me say I have reasons to be on the continent without being seen on any big ship."

The Hiziker smiled broadly. "I think you know quite a lot about what goes on down here on Eerie Island. There is a regular traffic that goes on during the late night hours. People go across, then return before dawn. I know the boats involved with such traffic. Nothing concerning it is hidden from my eyes."

"How many passengers can such a vessel hold?" eagerly inquired Scopo.

"Up to half a dozen, though the boat becomes a little crowded. But most people doing that don't mind being uncomfortable. Not at all."

"How many can your boat hold?"

The Hiziker made a grimace. "You want to take others with you? That is possible, but it would cost a lot more."

"The price means nothing to me. What I want to do is bring others with me when and if I decide to do so."

The boater scratched the stubble on his chin. "It will not be cheap. At least five hundred porizi."

"I can afford that amount," admitted Skopo. "Where and when can I pay you the fare?"

"Be here on this wharf at midnight, you and your companions. My boat will be docked nearby. I shall be able to fully accommodate you and anyone who accompanies you, my good man."

Part V.

20 MAR
IX.

The last persons to leave the Mesmeric Drama School were Teba the actress and the viroid technician, Tuko Tara. It was the latter who was locking up the main doors of the building as the pair were on their way out.

"There is no need to walk back to your hotel alone, Miss," said the man in charge of the ribbon masks. "I am going that way and I can accompany you if you wish."

"Thank you," she smiled, "That is very kind of you."

The two exited out to the late afternoon street scene and began to amble away from the school when Teba started to talk.

"I am happy to be here on Eerie Island, taking part in an important, promising project that holds great promise for progress in dramatic presentations, and you have an important role in all that we are involved in, but you never appear to have a part in the joy and satisfaction of the group, Tuko.

"Perhaps I shouldn't say this to you, but you seem a sad and despondent individual to me. Pardon me, but I have always been highly sensitive to the emotions of those around me, especially the people I work with.

:If you ever want to relate what is troubling you to someone else, Tuko, I am ready to listen, and I can often give good advice to others."

A period of silence followed as the two of them moved slowly forward.

At last, Tuko turned his face toward her. Both of them halted and looked at each other.

"There are aspects of what I am doing that bother me inside," he told her quietly. "They lie deep inside my mind every minute of every day."

"We can go into the café at the corner and talk about things, Tuko," she suggested with sympathy. "I have plenty of time to listen to you, my friend."

✦ ✦ ✦

The two men walked from the Colonial Hotel to the dock area as twilight fell over the harbor. Darker grew the blue shadows on the water. Night was quickly approaching.

Skopo and his companion stopped a little way from the bench where the Hiziker was to meet them. Mizo sat down while the detective remained standing, on watch for the appearance of their transporter for that evening.

"Here he comes," announced Skopo, catching sight of the movement of the boat-owner in the thickening dusk. The latter walked briskly toward the pair awaiting him.

"I am happy to see that you and your friend are here on time," began Hiziker as he came nearer, not making any kind of greeting beyond that statement. "Please follow me over to where my craft is tied so that we can board it at once."

With the mariner in the lead, the three figures advanced onto the beach and proceeded away from the boat docks. The light tubes of the harbor disappeared as shadows swallowed the group. The night sounds of island birds and insects came out of the woods that paralleled the shore. In a minute, they had left the port and the town in the distance.

A group of cottages suddenly appeared ahead of them. Their windows were lighted up. All at once, the four were inside a large, open clearing.

The Hiziker stopped and whispered to the two following him.

"We have reached the village where I live," he informed them. "Now, I will take you to my boat so that we can embark on it. I beg you to keep quiet and maintain silence as we go forward."

Their guide led Skopo and Mizo forward toward the water, only stopping where the shore sand began.

A loud, gravely voice called out as a flood of light went on from the deck of a vessel docked on a small pier. "Who goes there?" shouted someone on board.

"It is only the Hiziker here. I am escorting two new passengers for tonight's sea journey, that is all."

The handtorch emitting the light moved away from the threesome on land. "Come forward so I can see who is there with you," said the person holding it.

Something clicked in the mind of the detective, a voice from the past. Whose was it? he asked himself. Why do I think that I recognize it?

Only when the party of three reached the boat did the face of the one calling become close enough to be clear.

"Come aboard, you two," said the voice. "It has been some time since we met each other in Kalender, Inspector."

The circle had made its way completely around. Predo Atat stood on the deck of the boat, a handtorch in one hand, a pulser in the other.

In the small cabin of the boat, Predo searched the policeman and took away his pocket weapon.

Then, the Hiziker bound the hands and feet of the two prisoners in plastex binding.

Predo stood over their bodies lying on the floor with a gloating expression.

"Do not think that I was unaware of your presence on Eerie Island, Inspector. I knew it the minute you arrived from Plazh. It was inevitable that at some time we would meet. But who would have believed it would happen like this?

"My friend, the Hiziker, has always been eager and willing to make a little money on the side. But it was never expected that he should bring me the one who has been on my tail ever since the encounter we had back in Kalender.

"Remember the way we fought each other and how you defeated my brother at the Atat Language School? And how I was compelled to leave the city where I had lived and practiced hydro-medicine?"

The Hiziker untied the boat from its moaring and started the engine. The transporter was soon headed into Eerie Bay at a slow, even speed.

Predo Atat gave a command to the boatman standing at the tiller.

"Turn in at the city dock so that we can pick up the Readers waiting for us there," he said in a bold, confident tone. "We will have a full schedule of erasure raids in Plazh tonight."

❋ ❋ ❋

Revelation followed revelation.

Skopo maintained self-control, keeping silent as Predo boasted on about what he and his movement were up to.

"You may think me mad. That does not bother me in the slightest. I know what the truth is.

"Our actions against the ribbon industry of Plazh have been a big, spectacular success. The planet of Farmer will have to give up all use of viroids within the near future. The cost of continuing will become prohibitive. It will be easier to return to how things were before my grandfather discovered how to mobilize viroids for practical ends. Today, we Readers have almost destroyed the entire entertainment industry based in Plazh. There are no more drama ribbons coming out of any studio. All production has had to come to a stop.

"I know what is going on at the Mesmeric Drama School with the new viroid masks that apply hypnotic techniques. But the Readers will not allow such masks to spread further. We shall ruin this development in the bud, do not doubt that. We have the knowledge and the means to achieve exactly that. It will end what these mesmeric actors are involved with."

Skopo glared at his captor. "How do you find out so much about what goes on at the drama school?" he shot back at the other.

Predo seemed to gloat with malice. "I have my methods. There are people there who keep me informed on what transpires. Some of the acting pupils have become Readers and are under our orders. They will carry out what we command them to do."

"You have agents inside the place who serve you?" gasped the detective.

"You would be highly unhappy to learn who it is," smirked the doctor. "For now, though, I will allow you to keep guessing about that."

The boat drew up to one of the docks within the city harbor. The Hiziker cut the engine to a low, stable whine while a team of four Readers climbed aboard.

As Predo went forward to talk with them, Skopo and Mizo looked at each other.

Both of them noted how the group at the front of the boat looked toward the dock as a figure in a black coat and a mariner's cap leaped aboard the craft.

Mizo instantly recognized who it was. Skopo followed only a moment after the son gaped at the appearance on the vessel of his own father, the head of the mesmeric drama institution.

* * *

The father attempted to justify himself to his son.

"It had to be this way, Mizo. There was no alternative. You know how many times my drama school has been near bankruptcy. I had to find a secure way of financing what I was doing. A supply of new, additional money was necessary for me to continue.

"Classical Eerie drama has never been capable of paying its own way through public support. So, when the Atat brothers came to me

VIROIDS

several years ago with a proposal to work together, there was no other choice available to me.

"It was Zado Atat himself who offered me the viroid mask for use in the training of our actors. It was he who found and trained Tuko Tarn to work as the school's technical master. The price of this partnership with the Readers was to facilitate their raids and assaults on the ribbon industry in PLazh.

"There will soon exist a team of actors whom I myself have trained. They will be assisting the movement of the Raiders as their secret agents in the fields of drama and general entertainment." The father gazed wishfully at his son, the ribbon director. "You have to adjust and comply as I have, Mizo."

The latter gave Kanm a desperate look. "These are evil people, father," he pleaded. "Their promises have no value at all. It was foolish to trust them."

"No," argued the father. "The evil ones are those who grabbed hold of viroid memory from the original inventor, the grandfather of the Atats. They misused and exploited what someone else had discovered through his scientific research.

"Look at what the studio-owners of Plazh have done to our classical dramas through using viroid ribbons. The true use of viroids is exemplified by the new mesmeric masks we are using in our school. That is the legitimate, justifiable version of the new technology. And the Readers have proved themselves the true champions of the correct path of ribbon application.

"You must join with me on the side of the Readers, Mizo.

"You and your ally, the detective from Kalender, will have to join our alliance or suffer serious consequences."

"What happens to the two of us tonight?" asked Mizo.

Kanm looked away without giving an answer.

* * *

As the boat's motor grew quieter, then turned silent, the craft approached an isolated portion of one of the side docks of the city harbor.

The two prisoners, inside the cabin, witnessed Kanm leave them there and go out onto the front deck to supervise the taking on of a small group of Reader vandals prepared for the night's vandalizing of Plazh studio sites.

The Reader assistants steered the boat into a convenient berth alongside the weir as the new passengers from the town of Eerie moved to its edge, preparing to board in the silent darkness of the port at night.

The drama educator and the hydrophysician suffered a sudden, unforeseeable surprise as they waited for the first of the new crew to leap onto the open deck.

It was a person unknown to them, an unidentified stranger who immediately posed a visible danger. Who could it be? This sudden danger?

"Raise your hands in the arm and do not make any resistance," whispered a strange voice with a metallic ring to it. "You and everyone here is under arrest. I hold a pulser in my hand, as do all of my fellow officers."

Kanm and Predo instantly saw two, then three and four other dark shapes approach his vessel from the lightless dock.

"You and those on this vessel are surrounded from all sides on shore," shouted a strong and loud baritone voice. "I place all of you under arrest in the name of the police administration of this island. Do not resist or else you will suffer for criminal action in the fulfilling of an illegal enterprise."

The first officer, now on the deck of the boat, took control of the flabbergasted Reader in charge, frisking and disarming Kanm of a small pulser carried in his pants pocket.

The remaining confederates gave up at once, none of them daring to fight against what was happening to them.

Resistance disappeared without a scrap of speech or action.

In the cabin of the small ship, Skopo and Mizo had been inert witnesses of the capture and arrests.

It was the detective who ventured out to speak to the rescuers and relate that there were two unwilling prisoners there who happened to be anything but vandalizing Readers.

As soon as the chief officer caught sight of Mizo coming forth out of the cabin, he knew that the mainlander in front of him was telling the truth.

"Let's get off this boat and go to the station," said the policeman. "We can straighten out what has happened tonight and find out where matters stand."

Skopo and then Mizo found themselves escorted onto Eerie Island dry land.

X.

The investigator from Kalender and Director Mizo found Teba waiting for them at the Colonial Hotel when they returned there after long exchanges with the local police at their downtown headquarters.

Skopo invited the other two into the then empty dining hall in order to hold talk about the events of that evening.

Once the three were seated at a round table, the actress from PLazh began to explain her role in what had just occurred.

"The arrests tonight came about because of the revelations that Tuko Tama made to me at the Mesmeric School this afternoon. It all came out of him like some kind of avalanche. Once he began to tell the story of his own involvement with the underground vengeance movement, the unfortunate fellow was unable to stop what he was telling and exposing to me.

"Kanm Harn was the person who brought him into the invisible conspiracy. He chose Tuko as the one who had the knowledge and experience to bring the mesmeric mask into reality. At the same time, Kanm had enough personal influence over the technical expert to make him into a tool of the vandal conspiracy. Before he was fully aware of it, he was completely compromised by his first steps in services to those involved with viroid erasures.

"But Tuko came to suffer from a gnawing conscience. He found himself unable to justify the terrible attacks he had become involved in, for he had become a sort of scientific advisor to the Readers based on Eerie Island and elsewhere in the Peculiars. Tuko was becoming increasingly uncomfortable with what Kahm was ordering him to carry out for this destructive movement."

Skopo asked her a question. "Were you, then, acting as this man's personal confessor, Teba?"

She nodded yes. "It seems as if he had been waiting to find someone he could trust, in order to get this matter outside his own thoughts and emotions. I was the right individual there at the right time, it would appear."

Mizo then spoke. "My father fooled everyone in contact with him. But now he is in official custody and will be prosecuted along with Preto Atat and all the other Readers who were captured last night. They will no longer bring ruin and destruction to the viroid entertainment industry.

"I will see to it that the Mesmeric Drama School continues to exist and operate, as well as recording new ribbons using the hypnotic method of acting. I intend to combine the old with the new.

"Do you agree to assist me in these future projects and activities, Teba?"

She smiled with encouragement. "Of course I shall, Mizo," she promised him.

"I hope we have witnessed the end of Reader criminal damage," added the detective, his face shining with relief. "They illustrate how far feelings of revenge can carry the misguided. When the minds of impressionable persons are taken over by unlimited passions of vengeful resentment, they become capable of major crimes such as the vandalism that we have witnessed all over our planet of Farmer.

"But I believe that we have brought final defeat to the viroid madness tonight."

The End